The Mysterious

LEDGE

LOREN HALLORAN

*This book is dedicated to
my four wonderful children,
Megan, Rylie, Jordyn and Isaiah.
May you someday read this to your own children.*

Acknowledgements

Faria Ahsan

Graphic Design Artist

Narayanganj, Bangladesh

Fariaahsan8@gmail.com

CONTENTS

PART I:
LEARNING LESSONS

PART II:
THE DREAM

PART III: CREATING THE TOTEM

PART I:
LEARNING LESSONS

One

Will

Dust billowed up from behind the old blue Chevrolet pick-up truck as it rambled down the bumpy dirt road toward Lake Cowichan, making it impossible to see if you happened to be following behind. In the back of the truck, nine-year-old Georgy Walker and his dog Ben sat on either side of the box. They leaned out, faces to the front, allowing the wind to rush into their faces.

"Faster, faster," Georgy yelled to his Dad. Georgy's Dad carefully veered the truck left and right, not too quickly, just enough to frighten Georgy into staying put on the floor bed of the box.

Living out west made way for a healthy, rural kind of lifestyle. Kids were always happy and never seemed to be in any sort of trouble. Georgy was one of those kids. His dog Ben was his best friend. They had spent most of their lives together, as Ben had been in the family since he was a pup and Georgy a toddler.

The year was 1961. Lake Cowichan, located on British Columbia's beautiful west coast of Vancouver Island, Canada, is a small town made up mostly of loggers and farm homesteads. The town shops offered just about everything a person could need and the shop owners were always ready to oblige with a smile.

Lake Cowichan was a friendly little place to live. It was the weekend, and that meant taking the fifteen-minute trip over the dirt road into town to stock up on groceries for the following week.

So, here it was, another sunny Saturday as they pulled up in front of Miller's General Store. Georgy's job was supposed to be helping his Dad with the groceries, but he would always end up over at the counter looking at the hunting knives, dreaming of the day when he might buy one. Georgy looked closely at the various styles on display. "Keep off the glass" was printed in big, black letters on the front of the glass counter.

A good hunting knife was something small boys yearned to have. Heck, you could use it for just about anything in the country if only they didn't cost so much money. Since it generally only took Georgy's Dad twenty minutes to do the shopping, Georgy made the most of his time dreaming and wishing.

Soon enough it was time to go. Georgy's Dad loaded the groceries into the back of the pick-up. Another couple of minutes and they would be on their way home.

Back inside, Mr. Miller, the store owner threw some sacks of flour and sugar up onto the counter. Once a month he filled an order for an old man that lived on the edge of the local First Nations reserve. Mr. Miller's son, Jason would help him deliver the groceries by truck later in the day. Jason and Georgy were classmates and played together at school, but ever since Jason turned nine, his Dad had him helping out in the store after school and on Saturday. Sunday was the only day they could get together, but only after church.

Georgy's Dad called the dog, "Let's go, come Ben, get up here." Ben jumped into the truck, eager to get going. Georgy and Ben loved riding in the back of the truck. Georgy felt important back there, especially when seeing someone he knew and would wave happily to them.

"Do you think I could go on the delivery with you Jason?" Georgy asked. "Let me ask my Dad," Jason offered as he scooted away. "Dad figures that would be okay," Jason said enthusiastically upon returning.

"Say, that old man Mr. Williams only lives a couple of miles from your place. How would you like to earn a couple of dollars by delivering them to him yourself?" Mr. Miller asked. "Go ask your Dad, Georgy. Let's see if he's interested."

Georgy rushed outside to ask his Dad. "There's lots of room in the truck. I'd be delighted to lend a hand," Georgy's Dad replied. "You go and get yourself a treat, Georgy. I'll go load up the delivery items."

Georgy was allowed to buy himself an ice cream cone with a portion of the allowance he'd receive each week. Off he and Ben went to the ice cream parlour. Two scoops of strawberry ice cream was Georgy's favourite cone. Once he got it, he and Ben ran back to the truck to head for home.

The ride over the dirt road home was just as bumpy as the ride in seemed to be. Ben dashed from side to side, taking in as much of the cool wind as he could. Georgy licked his cone but saved a little to give to Ben, as he did each week.

They would be home in another couple of minutes. Georgy knew that once his chores were finished, he could play the rest of the day.

As they approached their home, Georgy thought of how bright the barn and toolshed looked. Georgy's Dad had been busy painting around the home and it looked great.

They drove up the dirt driveway and stopped in front of the porch. The sweet smell of freshly cut hay softened the dry, hot air that lingered amongst the forested area around their homestead. Georgy looked forward to some free time on the weekends. As long as his chores were done he could play all day. Right now he had a job to do. As soon as they unloaded the family groceries, Georgy anxiously piled into the back of the truck again, eager to get on with their delivery.

Ben couldn't go unless he was tied up in the back because Georgy's Dad didn't know if the old man liked dogs or not. Georgy's Mum came out onto the porch, "Lunch will be ready in ten minutes, so you had better hurry," she said. "The delivery is just up the road. We will be right back," Georgy's Dad replied. They drove about two miles over the washboard-like road until they reached the reserve.

The kids used to like to play there because the people were friendly and didn't mind the children around. During hunting season, the kids were allowed to watch the men skin the deer they'd shot. The children were fascinated by this.

Today, though, they didn't drive into the reserve. They stopped on the edge, out by the woods. There, alone amid the trees, stood a small wooden cabin. Smoke was coming out from a pipe sticking out from the roof. There was no driveway in, just a swinging gate that was hinged between two cedar trees about fifty feet away. There was a small painted sign that read "welcome". It was hard to read because the paint was faded and had chipped away in places. Funny, there was no fence, just a gate.

An old wooden chair with some freshly whittled shaving around it sat just outside the front door. Whittling was cool, Georgy thought. "I wonder what the old man might be carving," Georgy said quietly. They knocked on the door, but nobody answered.

Packing the supplies, the fifty feet wasn't easy. Dad and Georgy had to make two trips with the groceries. Just as they were setting the groceries down by the front door, it opened and the old man said, "Hello. I hope you haven't been out here too long. I was napping and hadn't heard you drive up."

Georgy noticed a beautifully carved knife handle sitting on a counter just inside the front door. The old man looked at Georgy and said, "You are not the boy that usually brings my groceries to me. Who are you?"

"My name is Georgy Walker, and this is my Dad."

"We were at Miller's store buying our groceries," Mr. Walker said. "Mr. Miller asked if we would mind delivering these to you. We are happy to help out since we only live a couple of miles down the road."

Georgy said, "I guess you could call us neighbours. There's nobody else living between your house and ours."

The old man asked if they would like to come in for some lemonade and rest their feet for a while.

"Can we Dad?" I'd sure like to see what you have been whittling. Did you make that?" Georgy asked, pointing to a knife handle.

"I have just about finished it. It is my favourite. I've been working on it for months."

"It looks awesome," Georgy said. "Someday I'm gonna buy myself one."

Georgy's Dad brought the groceries inside. "Georgy, remember what your mother said about your lunch. Only ten minutes, right? We have been over fifteen already," he said.

"Aw, Dad, can't we tell her we couldn't find the house? We'll only be a couple of minutes."

"Don't keep your mother waiting," the old man said. "Why don't you come back and I'll show you some of my carvings. I've got plenty."

Georgy's Dad nodded in approval to Georgy.

"Can I come back after lunch if it's okay with Mr. Williams?"

"Please call me Will. I've been everybody's Uncle Will for the last fifty years or so. You come back after your lunch and I'll tell you a story about a young boy who never wanted to do anything but carve."

Will winked at Georgy's Dad. "I won't keep him very long. By the way, what is that in your truck, a bear?"

"Naw, that's my dog, Ben." Georgy said. "He's a lab. He just wants out. Do you like dogs?"

"I used to keep one around to chase the raccoons away from my chickens. I gave up on chicken raising a long time ago. The last dog I had died about ten years back. I haven't had one since. Yes, I suppose I still like dogs, as long as they're not too rambunctious. It interferes with my work."

Georgy's Dad said, "Maybe you should leave Ben at home when you visit here."

"Okay Dad. We'll see you later after lunch, Will."

Will patted Georgy on the head and said, "Thank you for delivering my groceries."

Ben barked enthusiastically as they piled into the pick-up. Georgy's Dad turned the truck around and headed for home.

Georgy's Mum was waiting for them. "Any longer and I would have eaten without you two," she said. "I was about to come looking for you."

"Ma, we met the old man over on the Reserve," Georgy said. "He lives just inside the border in a cabin in the woods. He's about a half a mile away from the other folks. I think he likes his privacy. He carves, Ma. He said he'd show me his work. He invited me to come over after lunch was done and he'd tell me a story."

"I guess you have found a friend, Georgy." His mother said. "Maybe you could take Ben for a run when you go."

"No Ma. He doesn't like dogs anymore. They have to be looked after while he's trying to concentrate on carving."

"Well, don't be too long, Georgy. We've invited the Millers over for dinner. Dinner's at five."

As soon as he could, Georgy hopped on his bike and peddled back over the road, carefully avoiding the holes as best he could. Thoughts ran through his head.

"I wonder if he has a bearskin on the floor?" he said out loud.

Georgy can't wait to get there. He just had to see that knife handle again. Georgy grew more than anxious as he drew closer to Mr. William's cabin. He could almost feel the smoothened wood of that knife handle in his hands. As he pulled up through the trees, a look of astonishment came over Georgy's face.

There by the old wooden chair was a blanket with over a hundred small wooden pieces placed on it. There were horses, whales, birds, trees, more horses, Indian braves, teepees, cavalry soldiers and even some of the stores from Lake Cowichan. All were polished and smooth.

Will came out from the house. "Welcome back Georgy."

"Wow!" Georgy exclaimed. "Did you make all these things? Can I hold them? Are they very delicate?"

"You must treat them with utmost care." said Will. "They have taken me years to finish and they are very dear to me."

Georgy was amazed by all the detail that had gone into the little pieces. They only stood about four inches tall.

"Look at these horses. You've got all the different kinds here."

"That's because there are lots of different kinds in our world. I made them to represent a herd of wild horses tamed only to themselves, Georgy, and I made them so they could run wild and free, just like they used to. Everything you see here represents something that has meant a lot to me at one time or another."

"Why do you have trees here Will?" Georgy asked. What do they mean to you?"

"I have different trees, just as I have different horses. All trees are different. Look closely. Each tells a story of its significance to me. In time I will tell you the stories, but first I think there is something inside that just might have caught your eye while you were here earlier."

Will showed Georgy into the cabin. Georgy's eyes widened as Will handed him the knife handle.

"I plan to fit a blade into it after the handle is done." Will said.

It was a little large for Georgy's small hands to grip properly, but it was magnificent looking. Georgy could already tell what it was going to look like when it would be finished.

"Have you ever been asked for any of these?" he asked. Has anyone else seen these little carvings?"

"Georgy, I have never just given any of these carvings away. I have sometimes traded with people for something I've needed. In those cases, they had something in mind that they wanted made, so I would make it for them. Nobody ever complained."

"Can you make anything, Will?"

"Almost anything."

"What did people want you to make?"

Will thought for a moment, "Well, usually a raven or eagle mask. I've made a lot of things for Mr. Miller. I used to trade him for food and supplies. I have made him knives, walking sticks, masks and a few bows. He sells them in his General Store. Mr. Miller buys moccasins, vests and coats from the women here on the Reserve, too."

"Do you have a bearskin rug, Will?"

"Oh no Georgy, I don't believe in killing the animals. They have every right to walk this Earth as we do."

"But what about the deer and moose the others shoot and skin?"

"Georgy, they hunt for food to feed their families. The skins are made into clothing to keep them warm. They have gardens, beautiful gardens, where many vegetables are grown, but they need to buy feed for their cows and horses. They trade clothing and baskets for supplies."

"What is that big stick leaning against the wall? Is it a piece of wood that you'll start carving?

"No. I'll tell you what. You bring it to me, but be careful how you handle it. It is very fragile. Keep it upright, just like it is. Lift it very gently."

Georgy walked over to the wall where the stick was. It was about four feet tall, and about three inches wide. It looked like an old branch from a fir tree. Georgy picked it up and slowly walked over to Will.

"Sit down here, close your eyes and listen carefully."

Will turned the stick upside down. Immediately Georgy's eyes popped open wide as the stick made sounds of rain pouring all around them.

"It sounds like rain, Will. Can I try it please?"

Will handed the stick to Georgy. As he turned it upside down the rain sound happened again.

"Can you guess what it is called?" asked Will.

"No, I've never seen anything like this before."

"It's called a rain stick. It is meant to sound like rain when you turn it upside down. When you close your eyes you can imagine a rushing brook or a thunder shower."

"Where did you get it from Will?"

"I made it. It took me a long time."

"Will you show me how to make one someday?"

"My boy, you are so anxious to learn. You seek many answers to so many things."

"Your place is pretty cool, Will. Can I bring a friend over to show him all these wonderful things?"

"I would rather you didn't. The less people know the better. I value my privacy and I have a lot of work to do."

"Did Jason Miller ever know about your carving?"

Will shook his head. "He never seemed too interested. As a matter of fact, Jason never spoke to me when they would deliver my groceries. He always stayed in the truck. Mr. Miller was always pleasant. He's a likeable man. Does this mean you will be delivering my groceries from now on?"

"I hope so. Like my Dad said, we live so close that we might as well. We have to buy ours and take them home too. I'd have never met you otherwise, Will."

Two
The Story of Braveheart

"I said when you returned, I'd tell you a story about a boy who never wanted to do anything but whittle. Would you like to hear about him?"

"Would I ever! Can I play with the rain stick while you talk?"

"No Georgy. The only thing I ask of you is that you listen very closely to all I tell you. You must not be distracted during a story, because then you lose your concentration. If you remain silent and listen very, very carefully, the story teller will take you there and make you feel a part of the story. Can you do that for me, Georgy?"

"Yes, I'll try."

Many years ago, before there were any schools, there was a small native boy named Braveheart. He was a very curious young boy, about ten years old. His Grandfather was a carver. Every spare chance he had, he could be found standing beside his Grandfather, watching his every move. As he chipped away at the fallen cedar tree, his next venture in what had been a long tradition of totem carving in his family. Braveheart wanted so badly to help his Grandfather. One day he let him hack away on a fallen tree. Grandfather noticed that he was working up a sweat. The look on the young boy's face showed persistence. He was totally involved in his work. To Grandfather's surprise, Braveheart was indeed focussed on creating a face like a mask right from scratch in the raw wood that was set in front of him. Grandfather knew then that this boy had carving in his blood. He decided to take him under his wing and show him how to use the tools properly, to respect the other people's work, and to respect himself, as he would be seen through his creations.

Braveheart was a keen listener. He worked hours upon hours at whittling objects of wood into small creations of joy. It wasn't too long before Braveheart was working with his Grandfather, helping more than anything. His desires were large. He worked long hours, weeks on end, until the symbols on his own totem were roughly completed.

Now it would take Grandfather to start detailing before the finishing look would be completed. Grandfather would begin his day by getting up at four am. He told Braveheart there were many hours in a day that were unseen and often lost because people would sleep through them.

Braveheart asked what his Grandfather would do so early in the morning. Grandfather replied, "You come stay with me tonight. I'll show you."

It meant they would be in bed earlier. That night Grandfather showed Braveheart his whittling skills on a piece of wood. Braveheart again shared quality time with his Grandfather, careful to do just as he was told. He learned a lot by just watching him. He worked with such speed and precision. Braveheart respected his Grandfather and desired to have his talent so that he too, could be as respected.

"Your time will come, Braveheart. Someday it will be you teaching your Grandchild how to carve." Braveheart accepted this to mean he would be taught and guided by the best carver around. That was the most special thing that could happen to him.

Grandfather said it was time they should go to bed.

"How will we know when it's time to wake up?" Braveheart asked.

"I just know from doing it for so long." His Grandfather replied. "The sun won't be up yet, so we can start by having a good breakfast. You sleep here, boy. It's going to be a long day for you tomorrow. Get some rest."

Grandfather was asleep within minutes after saying goodnight to Braveheart. He found it hard to get to sleep. Thoughts of his Grandfather spending so much time showing and teaching him inspired him even more. Before long he dozed off for what seemed to have been only a couple of minutes.

"Braveheart. Wake up. It's time to get up, Son." He moaned and moved into a more comfortable sleeping position. "I just got to sleep," he complained.

"Get up, Son. I have some hot oatmeal ready for you. We have to get a move on. The sun will be up in half an hour."

Braveheart forced himself out of bed. "It's cold, Grandpa."

"Come and sit by the stove. There is a fire going now, but once it goes out, we have got to go, too."

"Where are we going so early?"

"We are going down to the river."

"To bathe?"

"No, Son, to fish. This is the best time of day to catch fish. It is so peaceful in the early hours of the day. Just you, the fish and the sounds of the water, interrupted only by the shrill sounds of the small birds as they fly about in search of their food. If you're lucky, you will see the eagle dive and catch his breakfast."

Braveheart began to think. This was going to be good. He ate his breakfast and sipped on some of his Grandfather's hot coffee.

"Better get a move on if we are going to catch any fish." Grandfather said. He stirred the ashes in the stove and took a long net from off the wall. As they set out for the river, daylight began to show its face, exposing drops of dew nestled on the blades of grass along the roadside.

"The river runs deep and its current is strong." Grandfather said. Do you know why the river is called Blackwater?"

"No, Grandpa." Braveheart replied.

"You will know once we get there".

A few dozen yards later they came to a path that led them down the bank to the riverside. There,

Grandfather took his position on a large, flat rock ledge.

"Come here Braveheart," he whispered loudly, "what do you see?"

"It is hard to see anything, Grandpa. It is very cloudy on the river. I cannot see the other side."

"Braveheart, the clouds you see are mists covering the river with a protective coating. It will linger until the warm sun causes it to disappear. Blackwater means 'River of Mists'. The early morning is a time when you might see other fishermen around you, yet you are alone. Fish use this daybreak mist to come to the river's surface to feed. The mist floats just a few inches above the river's surface and protects the fish from the birds. This is why I come at this time, Son. This is why my father came. He also showed me when I was a young boy. If you listen, you will hear the fish as they jump up into the mist and fall back into the water. They will sound like rocks being thrown into the river. Soon the sounds will be close enough for us to know to put our net in. As the sun warms the mist, it melts it from the bottom closest to the river's water, up until it has completely faded away. This is when my friends up high in the branches dive for their breakfast. We must hurry to catch ours before the mist is lifted, otherwise the river will be full of Kingfishers pelting the river's surface and scaring the fish away with their noise."

Braveheart looked up above them. "Look, Grandpa, there is the eagle. When will he take his turn?"

"He waits for the right opportunity. He rarely misses when he swoops down from his branch. The other birds stay clear of him in his fishing area. When the mist is almost completely gone, he will. His eyes are as powerful as his vision is strong. I see him dive through the remaining mist and catch the unsuspecting fish. That eagle watches me every day. Listen, Braveheart, the fish play around us. Watch how I use the net."

Grandfather slowly lowered the net into the water until the long handle disappeared. Careful not to make a sound, he then stirred it around slowly and then quickly brought it back up to the surface. As he lifted the net out and towards himself, Braveheart saw two fish inside the net, flopping around. They seemed as mad as hornets. Grandfather took a large knife and whacked them on the head with the handle until they stopped moving.

You see Son, the river is again kind to us. This time you try, but first look around. As the sun begins to shine on the mist the others will fish around us."

Just then the sun cast shadows of Grandfather and Braveheart against the white bank of mist, creating a dozen silhouettes of the two of them, fishing together in a large group. The warm sun was quickly beginning to burn the mist away. Braveheart smiled as he realized what his Grandfather had said earlier about seeing other fishermen even though you were alone.

"The mist plays tricks with us, Grandpa," he said.

Braveheart took his turn with the long handled net. It was difficult to balance because of its long length. Grandfather held the end as Braveheart dipped the net into the river. He didn't want the net to get away from the boy. At times the undercurrent beneath the surface could be quite strong. Grandfather had to use control when hanging on to the net due to the current pulling at it.

"Pull it up slowly, Braveheart, so as not to startle the fish." As the net reached the surface it showed they had caught nothing.

"Maybe they've gone, Grandpa."

"Try again, Son, but go easy. Try not to make any sudden movements. This time we'll stir the net back and forth, and then when I say so, bring it up fast."

They stirred until Grandfather gave the word to pull. "Now Son!"

They pulled the net up, and to Braveheart's surprise, they had caught another fish. There was only one, but it was larger than the two that Grandfather had caught. It flopped about like it was out of control.

"Hit it with the knife handle." Grandfather said. "Bonk it on the head. That's the only way you will stop it from getting away, otherwise it will fight its way back into the river or maybe even bite you good and hard in the meantime!"

Braveheart tried a few times to bonk that fish, but he couldn't get the fish to sit still enough to get a good aim at it. He dumped him out of the net. When the fish hit the rock he flopped angrily all around so that neither could stop him. Just as Grandfather was about to jam the net over the fish, Braveheart lunged to block the fish from flopping over the edge. The rim of the net hit Braveheart in the chest, knocking him off balance and into the river.

"Braveheart!" Grandfather shouted as he piled into the river after him. At the moment Grandfather jumped in, a huge bald eagle flew down and grabbed Braveheart by the arm guiding him over to the riverbank some fifty feet down stream. Grandfather couldn't believe his eyes. Frantically he made his way over to where Braveheart was. He found him shivering on the bank, but mad as ever at that fish.

"I'm going to hammer that fish Grandpa! I hope it didn't get away"

"Never mind the fish. Did you see what happened to you a minute ago?"

"No, I was too busy trying to get out of the current and to the bank."

"Son, it was all I could do to get out of that current just now. You were helped by the eagle. I saw him guide you to the shore, but where is he now? Why would he go? Let's get you home,

Son. It's pretty cold now."

Let's go back and get our fish first, Grandpa."

They climbed up the riverbank and ran back to the pathway. By now the sun had burned away practically all of the mist. As the two reached the rock ledge, they looked up in time to see the eagle dive down and lock its huge talons into a big salmon. It scooped the fish up and flew away over the trees, probably to his nest nearby.

> Braveheart noticed the net had fallen over his fish. He whacked it over the head and said,
>
> *"There! That's what you get for causing this to happen to me!"*
>
> *Grandfather hung the three fish on a stick that he had brought with him that morning. They made their way back up the path and onto the road. They were really cold when they got home.*
>
> *Grandfather wrapped a blanket around Braveheart. He quickly stripped out of his wet clothes and wrapped himself in a blanket. He then threw some wood into the stove and lit a warm fire.*
>
> *"That's not how I usually like to start my day, Son, but it worked out for the best. We are both safe and we have caught our dinner, too."*

"Will, what did Braveheart and Grandfather do for the rest of the day?" Georgy asked.

"Georgy, you've been here for nearly three hours. Won't your folks be expecting you home soon?"

"Dinner's at five, Will. We're having the Millers over for dinner after their store closes"

"There is a path that leads over towards your place, Georgy. I have travelled it hundreds of times. Before your home was ever built, I used it as a short cut to the river when I would go fishing."

"Will, I need to hear more about Braveheart. Will you tell me tomorrow, after church?"

"Sure Georgy, if it's okay with your folks, come back after your lunch. I'd be glad to tell you more about Braveheart. Take the trail tomorrow. It will save you some time. I'll tell you what, why don't you bring your dog? What's his name again?"

"Ben. Are you sure, Will?

"Yeah, as long as he doesn't mind running on a rope. I've got one that runs from this tree here over to where the chickens used to be, over there. That is about thirty feet. What do you think, Georgy?"

"That's swell! I'll bring him over tomorrow."

Georgy raced down the road towards home. He was in such a hurry to tell his folks that he hadn't even said thank you or good bye to Will. As he coasted up to the front porch he could smell potatoes and chicken cooking and noticed two freshly baked apple pies sitting up on the open kitchen window sill. Ben ran up to greet Georgy. Georgy let his bike fall as he dove on Ben to wrestle him. Happy to see Georgy, Ben jumped on him and licked his face wildly.

"Georgy, if that's you, you had better get in here and wash up quickly," said his Dad. "The Millers should be over any time now."

Just then Georgy heard a noise and noticed the Miler's truck winding its way down the road toward their home.

"They're here, Ma!" he shouted.

"Well, go get cleaned up Georgy," his Mum scolded. "You look like you need a good soak in the tub."

"I didn't even play over at Will's house. I just . . ."

"You heard your mother, Son. Hustle now. The Millers have arrived."

You could always tell when someone was coming, as Ben would usually start barking and then happily greet anyone who drove into the driveway. Georgy's Dad met the Millers at the front porch.

"How was business at the store today, John?" he asked.

"Fair today, Gus. Thanks for running that delivery out to Mr. William's place. It saved me time today."

"We didn't mind at all. He sounds like an interesting fellow."

"He's real weird," offered Jason as he looked up from petting Ben.

"Georgy didn't think so," said Mr. Walker. "He was so fascinated by some story-telling that he asked if he could go back after lunch. He was there for hours. As a matter of fact, he just got back a few minutes ago."

Just then Georgy raced out the front door.

"Jason! You wouldn't believe the carvings the old man has over at his place! He told me not to tell anyone, but you're okay because you've been there before."

"He's scary, Georgy. He'll tie you up and throw you down into the cellar! There are snakes in there, and there's no light. I've heard that once you're caught, you're never seen again."

"Who told you that, Jason?"

"The other kids at school. One time they were hiking over by his place and they were throwing stones at his gate. He came running out after them yelling he'd throw them in the snake pit if they ever showed their faces around there again. He told them he had lots of bad kids locked up in his cellar, and if he caught them that's where he'd put them!"

"He's just telling them that, Jason. He's very kind and seems pretty smart for an old man, too. He tells stories, Jason, and boy, you should have seen those carvings! He made a knife handle that is the best that I've ever seen. You know that he's even got a piece of branch that sounds like rain when it is turned upside down."

"Sure, Georgy. Anyway, you won't get me over there. I was glad when your Dad said you'd take his supplies over to him. I hated going there!"

"Come on boys," Georgy's Mum called. Jason, you go wash up and sit yourself down to the table. You can sit by Georgy."

"Ma, can Jason and I sit outside on the porch?"

"I suppose you could, as long as you don't fool around with your food or feed it to Ben."

"No way Ma! I'm super hungry and you know I like chicken and potatoes."

So, while the parents visited together inside, Georgy and Jason sat on the porch steps and wolfed down their food so that they could play. By the time Georgy's Mum came out to check on them, they were already in the barn jumping from the loft down into the hay below.

"I guess you don't need any apple pie." his Mum yelled.

With that the two boys bolted back to the house, racing Ben on the way. While they were devouring the two huge pieces of pie, Georgy again tried to interest Jason into going with him over to Will's house after church the following day.

"He's going to finish telling me the story he started today."

"I'm not going, Georgy. I'm going fishing with my Dad tomorrow. I'd just as soon never go over there, and neither should you, if you know what's good for ya."

"Well, I can't wait. He says he doesn't like dogs, but he said I could bring Ben next time. Did you know there is a secret pathway that leads to his place from here? It's supposed to be just behind the barn in the trees. Let's go see if we can find it! It won't be dark for a few hours, what do you say?"

"You're nuts! What if we get caught and tied up!"

"You're a scaredy cat, Jason. Let's just see if we can find it."

Georgy took off, Ben nipping at his heels. Reluctantly, Jason followed. "What the heck," he muttered to himself. "There's no harm in just looking for the path."

Three
Discovering the Path

The boys pushed through the light brush for about fifty feet, scrambling over old fallen down trees. Georgy shouted, "This is it! Look, you can tell a path was here before. It's kind of grown over, but there is a trail that goes in both directions. The old man said he used to walk it to go down to the river, and this path is headed right for it. The river is only about a half mile from our place. We've got to try this trail, Jason."

"No way, Georgy. Maybe next Saturday or something. It's six o'clock and we have to be getting on home soon."

"I'm going to get my bike. Let's go Ben."

Georgy took off. Ben scampered back through the brush. "How are you going to get your bike in here Georgy?" Jason yelled. "There are too many logs and bushes."

In a minute Georgy made his way back to Jason and said, "Yeah, right. I'll have to ask my Dad if he will help me cut a path into the woods so that I can ride."

"Why don't you wait until tomorrow and investigate by walking it? There might be tons of logs or tree roots in the way."

"Yeah. I'll take Ben and try it out after lunch."

Jason picked up a pine cone and threw it at Georgy, barely missing his shoulder.

"You're still a chicken, Jason."

"Maybe there are snakes on the trail and Indian warriors that are waiting to scalp you."

Georgy picked up a wet, hard packed pine cone and nailed Jason on his leg.

"Yeow!" Jason shouted.

The pine cone fight was on. Each picked a tree to hide behind for cover. Ben chased after the pine cones that missed their targets.

All of a sudden Georgy said, "Jason! C'mere, quick. Look at this." Georgy pointed to a spot on the tree beside him. There, Jason noticed a long bare spot of missing bark from one side of the tree. It looked as though someone had yanked a strip right off the tree. They looked around at the other trees and found that some had similar scars. They began to look more closely at the forest around them. As much as they had played in the woods as kids, they had never really noticed what the forest was all about.

"Georgy, the marks on the trees all seem to be in the same place and the same height. What could have made those marks?"

"I don't know, Jason. I've never played too far into the forest to have seen them before. Dad would only let me play around the tree fort he made for me just inside the trees."

"Let's get out of here Georgy. It's starting to look spooky here."

"Come on Jason. Let's see how many of these trees we can find. We'll only go up the path a ways. Ben will guard us. Don't worry!"

The boys gazed up at the large trees. Moss covered roots stretched out over the path making it almost impossible to ride a bike over.

"It's a good thing you didn't bring your bike, Georgy. You'd kill yourself in here."

"This is cool, Jason. Look at how big these trees are. There's another mark on that tree over there."

"Do you think bears made those marks, Georgy?"

"I'm sure they did. My Dad had to shoot a black bear a couple of years ago. It got too close to our barn."

Georgy reached up and touched the bottom of the scar. "It would have to be a bear to reach the top of this mark, Jason."

A big, black raven sat high in the branches of a tree beside them and began to caw noisily. Georgy and Jason both looked for some wet and heavy pine cones to nail him, but couldn't find any.

"He's too high up anyway, Jason. We'd never hit him."

The boys hadn't noticed, but they had wandered into a thick clump of dense forest. More ravens appeared in the branches and began to clamour about loudly, as if to complain of the boys' intrusion into their forest. Pine cones fell around the two boys. Ben barked and ran around trying to get everyone that bounced off the ground.

"Georgy, we're way in here. Let's get out of here before it gets too dark to see where we're going. These big trees hide the light from getting in here."

So, back they ran, racing each other. They were no match for Ben. He raced on ahead of them.

"Where do we get out of here?" Jason called, short of breath.

"The trees are thinning out now."

When they got to the tree fort, Georgy said, "Let's just head out here, Jason. Here Ben! C'mon boy, let's go."

Ben bounded over a log and thrashed his way through the brush. They ended up being just a few yards away from where they first went in. They ran to the porch to sit down.

"I'll get us some lemonade, Jason." Georgy said.

Inside the folks were still busy talking and laughing. They'd been friends for a long time. They had all been born and raised in the area and had gone to school together.

"Are you boys having fun?" Georgy's Dad asked.

"You bet, Dad." Georgy replied, as he and Jason gulped down their cool drinks.

"We found an old trail out past the barn that Will said he used years ago when he'd go to the river to fish. He says it will take me right to his house. Dad, are there bears around here? We found some really big trees with some patches of missing bark on them. It looks like bears might

have peeled it off."

"Georgy, why don't you wait until tomorrow and ask Will. I will bet he knows, Son."

"I'll do that," Georgy said. "Can we go back outside for a bit longer, Dad?"

"No Son. The Millers are going now."

"Well, I guess we should be leaving." Mr. Miller said. "We are going fishing before church tomorrow. Jason wants to show me how to fish. We'll be getting up pretty early, so we'd better get some rest."

As the parents said their goodbyes, Georgy and Jason talked more about their adventure.

"I'll take that trail tomorrow, Jason, and I'll tell you about it at school on Monday."

"I still think you are crazy to hang around that old man. And what if a bear gets you in the trail?"

"I think I'll take my bike in there tomorrow. It won't be that bad. Anyway, I'll have Ben with me for protection."

"Have fun fishing, Jason. I'll see you on Monday."

As the Millers left, Georgy waved goodbye. He turned to his Dad and asked, "Will you help me cut a path into the woods so that I can get my bike onto the trail?"

"You don't mean right now, do you Son?"

"No Dad, but I want to be able to ride my bike to get away from bears."

"There aren't any bears here anymore. The hunters have seen to that. They've done away with them. I haven't seen one since the one I had to shoot a few years ago. I don't think he would have bothered anybody, but he got a little too close to the house, and then got angry when Ben confronted him. Yes, Ben, you remember that big, old bear?"

Ben's eyes widened with anticipation that there might be another bear outside. He took off toward the barn, barking noisily as he ran.

"Oh, he remembers, Son. I don't think Ben's ever been threatened like that since. I'll tell you

what, Georgy. Let's get up early tomorrow morning and go clear the pathway for you. It shouldn't take us more than an hour."

"Thanks, Dad. I can't wait to start."

Georgy liked when the Millers would come for dinner. He wouldn't have to help his Mum with the dishes because the women enjoyed doing them together so they could catch up on what was happening in town. Georgy thought he might go to his room to lay down and think about Will's place, but two steps from his bedroom door, his Mum called him.

"Remember church tomorrow, Georgy. You had better get in the tub. I want that first and second coating of dirt off you by tonight."

Grudgingly, Georgy subjected himself to his once- a- week bath. He had to, whether he liked it or not. Georgy called for Ben to come over and visit with him as he suffered out the chore of washing.

"Make sure you scrub yourself clean, Georgy." His Mum called out.

"I know." replied Georgy, as he flicked drops of water at Ben who was attempting to ignore him by trying to snooze beside the tub. As Georgy finished his bath, he realized he would soon have to go to bed. It was nine o'clock already, so if his Dad was going to help him with the pathway, he'd have to rest up to be wide awake enough to be useful as a helper.

Morning came quick.

"Georgy, it's time to get up, Son. Let's get started."

Georgy flew out the bedroom door. "I'm ready, Dad, let's go."

"Hold it, Son. Your mother was kind enough to make you some breakfast. You will need your strength to pull the brush over to one side as I cut it away. We will only have about an hour, so we will have to work hard."

Georgy gobbled up his scrambled eggs and toast. With a final gulp of milk and a swipe with his shirt sleeve across his mouth, Georgy excused himself from the table, telling his Dad he would meet him out by the barn.

"Feed your dog, Son." His Dad said.

"Okay, Dad." Georgy replied.

Ben wagged his tail and licked his chops, knowing what would happen next. Other than winter, Ben had been staying outside on the porch at night over the last year. He was a good guard dog. Rarely did they ever have a problem with raccoons or a coyote since Ben was on the lookout.

Georgy knew the chickens were easy prey to the animals at night. On more than one occasion Georgy's Dad had to run outside with his rifle in the middle of the night to attend to squawking chickens being rustled. Owls and hawks posed the biggest threat, as they could fly in over the fence easily.

Georgy was filling Ben's bowl when his Dad came out on the porch. "Another beautiful day,

Georgy," he said. "How about giving the chickens some feed while I water the horse. Then we can start on your trail."

Georgy knew the routine. You couldn't just feed the chickens without collecting the eggs, so he took a tin pail that was hanging from a large nail just inside the door, and collected ten warm, freshly laid eggs that would certainly be devoured by breakfast the following day.

Ben ran around the outside of the hen house, scaring the daylights out of any chicken that was

stupid enough to let him. "It must drive you nuts not to be able to get in here, eh Ben?" Georgy teased.

As Georgy left the hen house, the chickens scattered out of his way. Ben made his way back around the pen and caused a frantic panic scene, with chickens flying everywhere.

"Settle down Ben?" yelled Georgy. "Here, go fetch!"

Georgy picked up a heavy stick and flung it some distance away. This gave him a couple of seconds to lock the gate and begin making his way to the front door before Ben could come back for more. This time Georgy threw the stick in the opposite direction to give him enough time to get the eggs into the house safely. Ben loved to nudge the pail as Georgy carried it, eager to see what was inside. Georgy hated when Ben would do this because he sometimes cracked the eggs when he bumped them.

When Georgy had put the eggs away he ran over to the barn. His Dad came out carrying tools and gloves. "You ready, Son?"

"You bet, Dad."

"So, where's your trail?"

"It's in there, about fifty feet or so."

"Fifty feet!" his Dad exclaimed. "I think I know the path you mean."

As they began hacking at the bushes, Georgy thought about going over to Will's later that afternoon. It helped to pass the time. For the most part the going was easy; mostly green bushes and light twigs that Georgy's Dad had no problem clearing away. There were only a couple of dead trees on the ground in their way and some low hanging branches that they eventually cut away. Ben kept himself busy sniffing around the pathway area. It wasn't too long before the task was done. They had finished clearing the trail in under an hour.

"So this is the trail that Will talked about, is it Georgy? You know, I used to shoot grouse back here years ago. There were times I thought I saw someone, but they would always disappear on me. I decided to stop shooting at the grouse for fear I might accidently shoot him."

"Thanks a lot for helping me, Dad."

"Glad to have been able to help, Son."

"Dad, I almost forgot!" exclaimed Georgy. "Will you come and see the trees that have the strips of bark missing?"

"Funny, I'd noticed them years ago when I was out here shooting grouse. Georgy, this was the trail I would use to hunt for them."

"Did you ever follow the path to see where it went?"

"Yes, it ends up at the Reserve just about a mile from here. It cuts off a good mile from getting there by road."

"Did you ever go to the river?"

"Georgy, Mr. Miller and I used to fish there when we were kids. You know, there *was* a man that would just be leaving when we'd get there, early on Saturday mornings. We would hide behind a large cedar tree and wait for him to go on up a trail. We figured this was probably his fishing spot we were stealing and that he would be mad if he ever saw us using it. He always had a couple of fish, yet there were times we would sit well into the afternoon and never get a bite. He must have gotten there pretty early to always be catching something. Either that, or he was just lucky. Listen, Son, we had better go wash up. We will be on our way to church soon."

As they made their way back over the freshly cut path, Ben ran up from behind them, brushing their knees and almost knocking Georgy off balance as he raced on ahead.

"Slow down, Ben" Georgy shouted. "He heard you say church, Dad. Look at him, he's headed right for the truck."

Ben knew that church meant a ride in the back of the pick-up. He danced around the truck, his eyes fixed on Georgy and his Dad, anxiously waiting for some sort of hint that they were actually going to get into the truck. Georgy and his Dad walked right by, paying no attention to him. With that, Ben sat down by the tailgate. He would just watch the front door and wait for some sign of movement. Sooner or later someone would have to come out and take him for a ride, and sooner or later someone did. About a half hour later the Walker family suddenly appeared on their front porch, dressed in their Sunday best.

MILLER'S
GENERAL
STORE

Four
The Walking Stick

Ben sprang to life. Georgy's Dad let the tailgate down so Ben could jump in.

"All aboard!" called Georgy as he scooted across the bench seat of the truck. Church would be fun today because Georgy couldn't wait to tell Jason the news of his path being cleared. When they arrived in town, Georgy noticed the Miller's truck parked outside their store.

"I guess the Millers won't be coming to church today, Dad. It looks like they just got back from fishing."

"The Millers never miss church, Georgy." His Mum said sternly. "They helped build this church and have only missed when one of their family members were ill."

Sure enough, only minutes after the Walkers arrived, Jason and his folks pulled up in their truck. Georgy noticed Jason sitting on his Dad's lap controlling the steering wheel. His Dad let him steer all the time.

"Hey, we saw you at the store just now." Georgy said.

"Yeah, we decided to get you an early birthday present, Georgy," boasted Jason. "Look in the back of the truck."

Georgy's birthday wasn't for another three weeks, so he couldn't imagine why he would be

getting a present now, especially from the Millers. He never got Jason a present last year. To his

surprise, he found a long, hand carved walking stick, or staff, as some people like to call them, lying on top of some blankets.

"We thought you could use this while you are out walking on that trail today, Georgy."

"Thank you for the present Mr. & Mrs. Miller," Georgy called after them, as they disappeared into the church. "Thanks Jason. I'll use it when I go after lunch." Georgy admired the work that went into the carving of the stick, with its smooth finish, and then set it back in the truck.

"So, did you show your Dad how to fish, Jason?"

"We only caught two, but I caught the first one. Had him worrying for a bit. He didn't catch his until just before we had to leave." Jason yawned. "We were up pretty early this morning".

"Jason, guess what?" Georgy interrupted. "My Dad helped me clear a path through to the trail. It's all done. Now I can take my bike in there really easy."

"No, Georgy. I told my Dad about the trail and about the roots that were sticking up.

He said you shouldn't ride your bike there, especially when there is not much light to see the ground properly. That's why we got you the walking stick."

"Yeah, you're right, Jason. If I did fall off my bike and crash, nobody would know to help me."

"That's right. Nobody but the bears, or that old man."

"Kids, come in please." Georgy's Mum called from the doorway.

"You stay put, Ben," Georgy commanded as they walked hurriedly toward the church.

Inside, Georgy and Jason sat on opposite sides of their folks. Although the folks sat together, there were fewer distractions when the boys were kept apart.

After church, Georgy proudly showed off his walking stick to his parents.

"That was very kind of the Millers," said Georgy's Mum.

"They got me this so that I wouldn't use my bike on the pathway."

"From what I remember of that trail, I would not ever use a bike on it. It is too dark to see the roots that have grown over the pathway in places," Mr. Miller said.

"I hear you're going to investigate the trail today, Georgy," Mrs. Miller said.

"Yes, Ma'am," Georgy replied. "I'm going over to Will's house after lunch to listen to the rest of the story he told me yesterday.

"Well, have a good time, Georgy," Mr. Miller said. "Jason's going to show me how to clean fish."

"No way, Dad!" Jason exclaimed.

"You've got to learn sometime, boy," Mr. Miller replied.

As they said goodbye, Georgy called to Ben. Lazily, Ben lifted his head over one side of the truck bed. He'd been having a nice, warm snooze in the sun.

"Can I sit in the back with Ben, Dad?" Georgy asked.

"No, you will get your clothes dirty. Jump in the front, Son."

Georgy couldn't wait to play with his new staff. He imagined himself as a fearless fighter of the trail, where no animal would dare mess with him. He told his Mum and Dad that now he could protect Ben when they would go out on an adventure.

Back at home, Georgy got changed and then sat down to eat lunch with his folks.

"When you are finished your lunch you may go to Will's." Georgy's Mum said.

Georgy finished up quickly and thanked his Mother for lunch. After excusing himself from the table, he went out to again admire the quality of the work that had gone into making the stick.

"Ben," Georgy called. Ben was out by the road sniffing around at something. "We're gonna go now, boy. I'll bet Will made this walking stick."

Georgy's Dad came out to the porch. "Take these ribbons with you, Son. Mark your trail so you won't get lost. Dinner will be at six tonight. Don't be late."

"I won't Dad." And with that, Georgy and Ben set off with his walking stick on the trail to Will's.

It was another beautiful day. The sunlight painted scattered patches of light on the dirt floor of the path as it struggled to push through the heavy branches of the thick forest of trees. Georgy whistled as he strode boldly up the trail. Ben cut on and off the path, checking out anything that moved, in some cases recognizing scents left by the boys being there from the day before.

Georgy passed by a small group of pine cones scattered among some dry leaves on the trail just ahead of him. He remembered the Ravens dropping them on Jason and him the previous day. It definitely got darker as they pressed onward through the dense forest.

Georgy marked some of the trees with the ribbons, and then tightened his grip on the walking stick as he jammed it forcibly into the hardened ground with each right foot forward step. Ben seemed to settle down and walked just in front of Georgy. Pine cones started to fall up ahead. Squirrels chattered noisily in the distance. Ben barked as an owl hooted nearby.

"Man, is it ever spooky in here, Ben," Georgy murmured.

Up above, a large Raven swooped down from the branches to get a closer look at the intruders. He perched himself in another tree close by, cocking his head to ensure he would notice their every step. Ben heard the noisy bird and wanted badly to go after him. The Raven taunted him by diving around, going from tree to tree. It drove Ben into a frenzy.

"Never mind him, Ben. He just wants to see who we are."

Georgy figured he would be about half way to Will's by now. He had an uphill climb to contend with. The walking stick really helped him as he climbed up the narrow trail. Over the years the trail had grown over in places, but Georgy could tell where the general direction of the trail used to go.

He cut bits of strips of ribbon and marked another tree, just to be sure. About another fifty feet from there, Georgy heard a rustling sound behind some bushes. He grabbed hold of Ben's collar.

"A bear!" he thought, as he held his breath, eyes wide open in their sockets. Just then a doe

leaped out of the bushes and upon seeing them, bounded hurriedly in the opposite direction.

Georgy held Ben back from chasing her. Ben barked uncontrollably at such a sight. This was right up his alley!

"That's all I need. You chasing the deer and leaving me to fight a bear all by myself. No way Ben, now settle down!"

Georgy slapped Ben's rump with a thwack of his hand. Ben's attitude changed immediately.

"Whew! Let's get going, Ben. That scared me."

Georgy scanned the area around and above him.

"That Raven disappeared, Ben. I guess he realized that we weren't a threat after all."

So, on they went. There wasn't one log in their way. The path was narrow but had been walked on enough in the past so that it remained relatively intact. To some extent, moss had covered the ground in places, giving it a carpet-like feel.

Looking around, Georgy noticed more of the same old scars on the huge trees around him.

"I've got to find out from Will just what happened to these trees to leave such marks," Georgy thought.

Birds chirped in the distance, giving the forest an almost relaxing edge to the already peaceful atmosphere. Georgy kicked at some large dried leaves that lay in his way. If he kicked them just right, by getting his toes under one side, the leaf would fly up in a partial circle, enabling Ben to scramble after it.

"I wonder what you'd do if you ever got into the hen pen. You'd be in your glory, wouldn't you boy?" Georgy said as he stopped to hug the dog.

Ben licked at Georgy's face. His tail wagged happily. You would never want to get hit with Ben's tail when he wagged it like that. It was so strong that it was like a thick rope when it hit you especially if he got you in the head. Ben is definitely Georgy's best friend and Georgy is Ben's. They had grown up together and had played together for years.

Georgy noticed the trees beginning to thin out a bit, just like at his house. Up ahead he could make out the side of a small cabin.

"That's got to be Will's place, Ben. Let's go!"

They ran the last part of the trail. It got lighter out as they came to the end of their journey.

Five

Back at Will's

As they approached the cabin, Georgy grabbed hold of Ben's collar and walked him up to the front door. He had to catch his breath from running. He waited a few more seconds then knocked. No answer. This time he called Will's name as he knocked. Still nobody came. Just then Georgy heard a chopping sound coming from the other side of the cabin. Georgy led Ben around to the back and called out again.

"Hello Georgy," came the response. "Come and help me carry this wood over to the cabin, would you?" Will asked.

"I've got Ben with me, Will, is that okay?"

"Sure," Will answered. "Come here, boy."

Ben took off in the direction of Will's voice and within seconds Georgy heard Will talking to him. Georgy ran over to say hello.

"Did you take the path, Georgy?"

"You bet we did, Will. It sure gets spooky. It's dark and quiet in there."

"What have you got there, boy?" Will asked as he noticed the walking stick in Georgy's hand.

"This is a walking stick, Will. The Millers gave it to me as an early birthday present because I was walking up the path today. It really helped, especially when I had to climb the hilly part. Did you make this, Will?"

"I sure did, Son. When is your birthday?"

"It's not for another three weeks, but I'm sure glad they bought it for me."

"Your dog is tired, Georgy."

"We ran the last part of the trail. He could probably use some water. Can I give him some, Will?"

"Sure. I think we could all use a drink. I've been chopping wood for an hour or so. I've just about had it too."

Ben curled up in some shade and rested as Will and Georgy made a couple of trips packing wood over to the cabin.

"I'll stack it later, Georgy. Let's go into the cabin and get a drink."

Will poured some water into a bowl and took it to Ben. He lapped it up eagerly.

"I'll put Ben on the rope now, Georgy."

"He won't mind, Will. He'll have a nap. It'll give us some time to finish the story from yesterday."

"Yes, come and sit outside in the shade."

Will fastened the rope to Ben's collar. Ben didn't seem to mind at all. He began sniffing the area, noting all the various smells. That was perfect. Soon he curled up for a rest.

"That should keep him comfy for a while." Will said.

He took a seat at the table under a tree beside Georgy. Together they sipped on cups of cold water that Will had dipped from a large wooden barrel. Will said each day he would take a bucket and fill it from a nearby mountain stream.

"Do you see that mountain, Georgy?" Will asked, pointing.

Georgy looked to where Will was pointing and noticed he pointed at the same mountain that he had stared at and wondered about several times over the past few years.

"Sure, Will, I've seen it lots of times."

"Well then, just you listen. Now back to our story."

Braveheart and his Grandfather got themselves dried off and warmed up. Grandfather said he'd pack some food and take Braveheart for a hike and a picnic.

"Let's go, Son," Grandfather said to Braveheart. "It will take us an hour or so of hiking to get where we want to go."

"Where to, Grandpa?" Braveheart questioned. "Aren't we going to carve today?"

"There will be lots of time to carve, Son. I'm taking you to a place where my Grandfather took me as a child, up to the top of the mountain. There I will share with you the treasures I was exposed to as a young boy."

Grandfather packed some bread, fish and corn in a canvas sack and poured water into an old canteen. He took some knives, a bow and some arrows from the wall.

"Let's go, Braveheart."

This was certainly proving to be an interesting day for a young boy. He looked up at the mountain and said, "I guess this should be exciting as long as I don't fall off the side of the cliff, right Grandpa?"

"One accident is enough for one day, Son. Besides, you won't have me bumping you with a net this time."

Braveheart found the mountain trail to be a challenge. Grandfather, on the other hand, had no problem at all. He had obviously done this hike a number of times before, and was in pretty good shape for a man of his age. Grandfather pointed out the different bushes with berries, mushrooms and trees that all lived together on the mountain side. He taught Braveheart which berries and mushrooms were okay to eat, and which ones were poisonous. He taught him many things about the trees, like their condition of health, age and the various insects that pestered the tree bark, causing the trees to become sick and look terrible. When they reached the top, Grandfather took his canteen from around his neck, took a big swig, and then passed it to Braveheart.

"Tastes pretty good, Son, doesn't it?" Grandfather said with a grin. "Come, follow me. I want to show you something."

Grandfather led Braveheart to the edge of the cliff at the very top of the mountain.

"Look down here, Son," he said.

Cautiously, Braveheart looked over the edge to see a land, rich with beauty.

"This is why I come here," Grandfather said. "To be around all that is beautiful. It was here that I created my first carving, lit my first fire and hunted my first Deer. You see the big tree by the ledge? It has a hole through its branch. It is where I sat with my Grandfather and listened to him tell me stories of the Elders for the very first time. Let us rest a while and eat. We will need to build a fire, Son. You gather up some twigs and moss and I will get some of the food ready.

When Braveheart returned, he set everything down into a small pile. Grandfather took two sticks and rubbed them together on a rock until some tiny yellow sparks flew onto the moss and twigs. Grandfather blew on the sparks until a small flame appeared and started a fire. Braveheart added more twigs to help the fire along. They were going to need more wood, So Grandfather added some dry, broken branches that were scattered around the area. Soon the fire got going quite well on its own.

Grandfather set some rocks and sticks into the fire. He then took his knife and two fish out of his pack and cut them up into even portions. He washed them with a little water from the canteen and placed them on the big rocks in the fire. Braveheart was impressed. The lighting of the fire was something that might take him a long time to master.

"I want to show you something, Son, while the fish is cooking."

Grandfather reached for his bow and arrows. He set a small piece of burlap sack over a tree stump. He then walked back about thirty feet and took aim. With great poise he drew back on the arrow, holding very steady before letting go. The arrow whizzed by in a perfect straight line toward the stump, striking the target in the middle of the sack.

"Wow, Grandfather, how did you ever learn to shoot an arrow like that?"

"It took a lot of years to perfect the art. To hunt with this weapon, one must be sure of where the arrow will strike. Otherwise, you will not kill, only wound and cripple the animal you hunt."

Braveheart was mystified by his Grandfather's wisdom and abilities.

"Someday you will hunt, fish and carve like I do. You will show your young how to start a fire from sticks and stones."

"I want to shoot the arrow. Can I try?"

"You hold the bow out with your left hand. With your right hand, hold the arrow tight to the string. Pull back on the arrow, making sure the bow stays as steady as possible."

The tension on the string was such that Braveheart could not pull back without losing the grip from his other hand.

"I can't do it yet," he said.

"No, not yet, but you will learn over time, Son."

The two sat down to eat a lunch of cooked fish, bread and water. When they were through eating, Grandfather suggested they have another look at the scenic view before leaving for home.

Together they talked as Grandfather shared stories of previous visits that he and his Grandfather had beside the big Cedar tree, over the years gone by. As they packed up, Braveheart thanked his Grandfather for taking him there.

"Boy, this sure has been a fun day," he said as he hugged his Grandfather.

"In time this will be a place that you can come to and call your very own. Just you and the wild, Son."

Using some water from the canteen, they snuffed out the fire completely. They turned and set off down the mountain trail for home.

When Braveheart and his Grandfather got back home, they began to work on the totem together. Grandfather showed Braveheart how he went about putting the finishing work on the totem. It didn't look easy. Once again, Braveheart saw that this, too, would take a long time to master. He was a determined young boy with potential. His Grandfather saw that in him.

Braveheart didn't mind waiting to be trained because he was being taught by the best. After a couple hours it was time to call it quits. Braveheart was tuckered out. It had been a long, but very rewarding day for him. His Grandfather told him to get some rest. "You will find me here first thing in the morning if you want to continue learning."

"Thank you, Grandpa." Braveheart said as he yawned and rubbed his eyes." I'll see you in the morning." Braveheart dragged his feet all the way home where he went straight to bed. He didn't even have enough energy to eat all his dinner.

"So, you see Georgy, Braveheart learned to respect his Grandfather's mind and abilities over that couple of days. That mountain that they climbed is the same one that I climbed many times as a young boy. It was my dream to one day join the eagles by climbing to the top of that mountain."

"Some days the clouds hovered in the thick of the trees. When I climbed the tree with the hole in the branch, I could look down on the clouds. The sun would be shining above the clouds. It was like being in an entirely different world. Sometimes I would sit up in the top of that tree until the sun would burn away the clouds, or the light winds would gently move them away. You know that there were days when an eagle would fly around up there, above the clouds. It seemed like it was just him and I up there Georgy, because I couldn't see anything else but us and the clear, blue sky. I would call to the eagle. He would always ignore me, but I knew he had seen me sitting there between the heavy cedar branches. I certainly never scared him either."

Will got up to get them both some more water. Georgy thought to himself how much he'd like to do what Braveheart did. One of his favourite places to play was in a field of clover just across the corn field from his house. He and Ben would chase each other, wrestle, play fetch, or chase butterflies or birds, whichever there happened to be lots of on any particular day. That's where you'd probably find him after school on a sunny day or possibly in his tree fort. He'd only hang out there if Jason was with him because Ben couldn't climb up there. They'd slept many a warm summer night up there, undisturbed in their private setting, up high in the tree. When it was just Ben and Georgy, they'd take off over to the field of clover, mainly because they'd be out of ear shot when his folks were trying to call him to hornswoggle him into doing chores. He'd stay away for hours. Georgy had admitted to his Mum that he's spent hours watching the mountain that was situated on one side of the field. He'd lie on his back and watch the clouds form various shapes as they passed overhead. Sometimes they'd get lucky and see an eagle soar high in the sky, circling above a tall Cedar tree near the edge of a cliff.

When Will came back he said that Braveheart and his Grandfather visited the mountain lots of times together. He said they began to see that other people had been visiting up there and were leaving trash behind and cutting the branches for fires. One careless fire could lead to total destruction of the mountain, so they decided to build a barricade of thick brush in a ditch near the top of the mountain, to keep people from going any further.

It took a long time, but eventually they succeeded in keeping people away from the mountain top. "I haven't been up there in a long time but the barricade they built was a pretty good one," Will said. Georgy remember the trees in the path. "Will, did you ever see the strips of bark missing from the big trees in the forest down the pathway?"

"Yes, Georgy. My folks and Grandparents used to tear the long pieces of bark away to use them to make baskets and mats to use and sell or trade for things they so badly needed for their own everyday use. They only used the bark from the red and yellow cedar trees."

"Will, did you ever see kids on the path when you'd fish so early in the morning?" "Yes, on a number of occasions I would see them come down that path as I would be getting ready to leave. They would hide behind a tree. They never knew that I saw them. They thought they were pretty sneaky." "Do you know who they were, Will?"

"Yes, Georgy, one was your Dad. The other was young Mr. Miller. By the way, Georgy, your Dad was a pretty good shot when shooting Grouse."

"He said he'd think he'd see someone, but they'd disappear, so he decided he'd better not shoot anymore. Maybe I'll get my Dad to teach me how to shoot."

At that moment, Ben started to act up. "I guess we should be going soon, Will. It gets pretty dim on that path." "Look at this first, Georgy." Will went inside and brought out the knife handle. "Last night I fit two pieces of white bone into either side of the handle, and was just sanding them down before I remembered I had some wood to chop. That is my daily exercise, Georgy, that and filling the water barrel outside."

"Don't you fish anymore, Will?"

"I haven't had to in a few years. The people on the Reserve are constantly bringing food over to me. They are just being kind, but they are also constantly bothering me."

"Maybe we can go fishing together, Will," hinted Georgy.

"How early could you get up to go, Georgy?"

"How's six o'clock?"

"No, the fish have been and gone by then. Try four am next Sunday. That way it will not interfere with your Saturday chores and you will not miss church either on Sunday morning."

"You're on, Will! Just like Braveheart! We'll see you next week."

"You are welcome here anytime, Son. Say, why don't you come after school on Tuesday and help me with my hunting knife. I will be fitting it with a blade by then."

"You bet, Will. Come on Ben, let's hit the dusty trail."

"Georgy, are you not forgetting something?" Will asked, pointing to Georgy's walking stick.

"Oh yeah! I wouldn't leave without that," Georgy replied.

"I am going to rest now, Georgy. For some reason I can hardly keep my eyes open."

As Will lay down on his cot, Georgy walked over to pick up his walking stick. He noticed a small box of wooden matches sitting on the counter Georgy had an idea.

"See you Tuesday, Will," Georgy said.

Georgy set off down the path; Ben was already yards ahead of him. About fifty feet into the trail, Georgy stopped and called for Ben. There was a small clearing and Georgy wanted to try something he remembered Will telling him about, when he was a small boy. He learned how to make smoke signals with the smoke from a fire. Georgy thought he would try it for himself.

"Maybe I will surprise Will," Georgy said to Ben.

He gathered up some dry twigs and moss then lit a match. He blew on the sparks turning them into flames. Georgy added some small dried branches and the fire grew. He had intended on using his coat to fan the flames into some kind of smoke signals but the fire began to singe the dry moss around him.

At that very moment, Will rushed by Georgy and, with a horse blanket, quickly snuffed out the fire. After a few seconds Will breathed a huge sigh of relief. Shaking his head, he looked over at Georgy and said, "That was a close call." Will wasn't mad but he was disappointed in Georgy.

Georgy was so embarrassed. He handed the matches to Will and said he was sorry for taking them. He had only wanted to impress Will, not start a large fire.

Six

The Hand Carved Knife

The trek through the trail went smoothly. Georgy had no trouble seeing which way he'd come. There were obvious signs where they had disturbed the otherwise neatly untouched leaves and moss on either side of the path Part of the way back was downhill which made it even easier going home. There were no signs of any raven, deer or squirrels. Georgy had seen all of the ribbon markers he had put up so he wouldn't get lost. In twenty minutes they were home. Georgy noticed his Dad working in the barn as he walked by.

"The trail was great, Dad. It was a lot quicker than going by road and more fun, too. You know what, Dad? Will remembers seeing you and Mr. Miller on the trail, and you hiding behind the tree when he was fishing. He even told me about you shooting Grouse on the trail."

"So it *was* him," Georgy's Dad said. "Well, we were pretty young then, about your age. That was a long time ago."

"You were able to shoot at my age, Dad? I wish you'd teach me how to shoot sometime."

"In due time, Son. Wait until school is out this summer, then I'll show you, okay, Son?"

"Thanks, Dad. I promise I'll be very careful with the rifle."

"There is a lot to learn first about safe handling and how the rifle works before you can shoot it, Georgy."

"I know, Dad, safety first, right?"

"You bet, Son. You had better get cleaned up for supper, Son. Go in and tell your Mum about your day at Will's."

Monday morning, as Georgy sat on the bus on his way to school, he thought of what he'd say to Jason about the path. Georgy saw Jason at the bus stop, talking to some other boys. As he stepped off the bus he noticed Jason quickly turn away as the other boys began to snicker.

"What's going on, Jason?" Georgy asked as he joined the group.

One of the other boys said, "You've still got your hair. We thought you'd be scalped or tied up and thrown into the old man's snake pit by now." They all laughed as they turned to walk into the schoolhouse. Georgy paid no attention to them. He knew better. Jason did, too, and he was supposed to be his friend.

"Thanks, but no thanks!" Georgy said to himself.

For the rest of the day, Georgy was teased and heckled by the other kids at school. Word quickly spread of his "stupidity" at wanting to spend time with a crazy old man. Georgy was pretty fed up. "Jason, you better keep your mouth shut or else I'll have to shut it for you!" Georgy said angrily. "Go ahead and try," Jason retorted. He acted pretty tough around everyone at school, although it wasn't like him to be so cruel.

"I was going to invite you over to see what we did on the path, but I guess you're still too afraid of bears, Jason. Just like the other day."

"Nobody cares about your stupid path. Have fun playing by yourself," Jason said sarcastically.

On Tuesday, back at Will's, Georgy told him about what was happening to him at school.

"Do not worry on my behalf, Georgy. The fewer kids I have nosing around my property, the better I like it. Besides, I have the best kid of them all with me, right now."

"Thanks, Will. I kind of like visiting with you, too. Those kids don't know what they're missing." "It is too bad, really," said Will. Do you think they are just jealous because you've found a new friend?" "Yeah, probably," Georgy answered. "Jason sure was mean to me in front of the other kids at school."

"Georgy, he never made an effort to be nice to me either, but you should always look for the good in people. Most often you will find it. Remember that Georgy, because it tends to bring out the good in you, too. Hook your dog up to the rope and come inside, Son."

Georgy did so, and then followed Will inside. There on the table lay the knife. Will had sanded the bone down flush with the wood so it looked like one piece. It was smooth and looked so beautiful. Will went to the window and a ray of sun reflected off the blade. The glare got Georgy in the eye.

"Wow, that's bright!" he exclaimed.

"It is very sharp, too." Will said, as he seeped glue into the cut out front slots of the handle. He took the blade and carefully wedged it between the slats in the wooden handles, then took a thin, rounded strand of leather that looked like a worn necklace, and wound it around the butt of the blade, binding it in tightly. Georgy was astonished at how good it looked. It was ten inches in length, of which six inches was a gleaming steel blade. "What do you think, Georgy?" Will asked.

"It's beautiful, Will. You are good at so many things."

"I hope I will be as good at fishing Sunday morning. Maybe you could meet me Saturday as

well, after your chores. You seem interested in the trees and their uses. We could walk the trail

and I will explain them to you."

"Would you? I would love to find out more about the missing strips. How long before you can use the hunting knife, Will?"

"The glue should be dry by tomorrow, but I'll let it sit tight until we fish on Sunday. Besides, I need to make a sheath to carry it in."

"How will you do that, Will?" Georgy asked.

"I will cut and sew some hard pieces of leather together and hang it on some pieces of leather

string attached to my leg or waist or wherever I decide to wear it."

"I wish I could do what you do, Will."

"You have lots of years to catch up, my Boy. Don't forget that I'm an old man, Son. What do you want to be when you grow up, Georgy?"

"I'd kind of like to be a person that looks after the trees and animals, Will. My Dad says I'd be good at it. He just wanted to farm. That's boring to me. I would like to work away from the house."

"Maybe so, but farming is still a necessary and important industry in today's time. It keeps a lot of people fed." "Will, when you and I go fishing, should I bring Ben along?"

"No, he will scare the fish. We need it as quiet as we can get it."

"All right, I'd better be going, Will. The knife looks really great."

Georgy unhooked Ben from the rope. "Thanks Will and goodbye," Georgy said, as he set out on the path. He carried his walking stick like a soldier, pointing at things and mimicked shooting them.

"You are a pretty good kid," Will thought to himself. "See you Saturday," Will shouted as Georgy was disappearing down the path. Georgy turned and waved as if to say okay, then quickly vanished into the thickening forest.

 For Georgy, Saturday seemed to take forever to come around. School was, for the most part, so-so. Jason could tell something was up with Georgy. He seemed to have this preoccupied

look about him in class. He thought he'd better make an effort to make friends again, because Georgy was his best friend and he really missed talking with him at recess and lunch times. Jason waited for class to be dismissed, and then said sheepishly, "I haven't treated you very nicely the past few days. I'm sorry."

"You're right," Georgy retorted. "You guys have been pretty mean by ganging up on me. You can say what you want about Will because I know different. As for Will, he could care less what you think or say. I've had more fun over at his place than you'll ever know!"

Some of the boys walked by and snickered at Georgy talking to Jason. "Shut up, you guys," said Jason. "Oh, now you're his friend, eh Jason? Hope you both get scalped." The group of boys laughed as they walked away. "See what you started, Jason?"

"I'm sorry, Georgy. So what *have* you been doing? Tell me about the path."

Georgy brought Jason up to date with his goings on at Will's. Soon it was time to get on the bus. Georgy was the last one on. The driver revved the motor and swung the door shut. Georgy waved to Jason through the window as the bus slowly left for home.

After saying hello to his Mum and Dad, and wolfing down a quick snack, Georgy decided to take Ben over to the clover field for a little fun. It was sunny out and he really didn't want to hang around the house. His Mum would keep him busy doing chores if she saw him doing nothing.

All Georgy had to do was change his clothes and he was out the door. It took only an hour of running in the hot afternoon sun before the heat took its toll on Georgy and Ben. They assumed their positions on the field, Georgy on his back with Ben sprawled out just inches from him. They waited patiently for the odd, small gust of a breeze to cool their faces. Georgy watched the slow but steady movement of the clouds as they gracefully made their way over the mountain top. Georgy focused on the tree on the edge. It looked like the ones he'd seen in the path. Funny, it was the only one of its kind up there. The others looked different. He'd make sure to ask Will on Saturday. He'd know for sure what kind of tree it was.

"Ben," Georgy said, "One day we're going to climb up there. No, I mean *I'm* going to climb up there. You'd fall off the edge in your excitement. I want to be like Braveheart and be adventurous by being up there. Maybe someday, Will can take me." A few minutes later Georgy got up and told Ben they had to go. "Dinner is probably ready, and I need some water.

How 'bout you, Ben?"

Ben wagged his tail and nudged Georgy playfully.

"Let's go home, Ben."

Saturday came with a fast start. Georgy was up extra early. He did his chores to get them out of the way, but the family still had to go to town for groceries. Georgy couldn't wait to go to Miller's store. He wondered if they'd want him to deliver anything out to Will's. He told Ben to pile into the truck. Georgy rode in the back with him all the way to town. When they got there, Georgy found Jason outside, sweeping the walkway.

"Got anything for Will today, Jason?"

"No Georgy. That's only once a month that we deliver to him. It's only been a week."

"Oh well, I'm going over there later on anyway."

Georgy's Dad led the way as they went inside to stock up. Georgy immediately went over to the walking sticks and other carved items that were placed by the counter.

"Are you enjoying your walking stick, Georgy?" Mr. Miller asked.

"It's perfect. Thank you, Mr. Miller. I've used it a few times on the path already. Will sure knows how to carve, doesn't he?" Georgy asked. "He is the best around. I have some of his work at home. Jason says you've been visiting him lately. He says you have become good friends."

"He's so smart. He tells me stories and I watch him work. He's just made a hunting knife that is the best I've ever seen."

"Please tell him I am interested in looking at it, okay, Georgy?" Mr. Miller asked.

"I'd better go check on Ben now. As soon as my folks are done I get to buy an ice cream for the ride home." "Have fun, Georgy," Mr. Miller said.

As usual, Georgy rode home in the back of the truck with Ben. And as usual, Georgy saved the last part of his ice cream to share with Ben. He'd been doing that for weeks. Ben just loved strawberry ice cream.

When they arrived home, Georgy pleaded to go to Will's, but his Mum said not until after lunch. Lunch wouldn't be for about an hour, so Georgy decided to get a jackknife that his Dad had given him, and practice throwing it against the barn. The problem was, he could never get it to stick in. Georgy imagined himself being a tough cowboy who could throw a knife into anything he wanted to, and never miss. He tried a few more times, and then gave up.

"I bet Braveheart's Grandfather could throw a knife," Georgy said to himself as he bent down to pick the knife up off the ground. Just then, Georgy's Mum called him for lunch.

"Yahoo!" Georgy shouted as he headed toward the front door. "Dad, could you ever throw a knife at something and hit it?" Georgy asked as he examined the jackknife in his hands.

"I got lucky a few times, Son, but it takes practice. You could never hit anything with that knife. A throwing knife is balanced. It is made to throw, and it usually has a longer blade. The Indians used to be quite good at it. In the olden days they used tomahawks, spears and knives to battle. You can bet they were good with their weapons, but they worked hard at learning how to use them."

"Will just made a big hunting knife. He's going to bring it fishing tomorrow."

"Did you say he was going to teach you about trees, Son?"

"Yes, he did, Dad. He told me a little about the trees that are missing the strips of bark. He's going to teach me more about them today when we walk through the path."

"It sounds to me like you are going to learn lots today."

"I learn a little bit every time I visit him."

Georgy finished up his lunch and made for the door.

"Have fun, Georgy," his mother said.

"I will," he replied. Georgy called for Ben. Together they made their way over to Will's cabin. Georgy noticed the different kinds of trees as he walked up the dimly lit path. He began to think about how people could possibly make things from the bark of trees.

Seven
Lessons of the Trees

Before he knew it they had arrived at Will's. Will was out back chopping wood again. In the near distance, Georgy could hear the dull thwack sounds of the axe splitting the wood. So could Ben. He took off behind the cabin to find Will.

"Hello Georgy," Will called, as he noticed Ben approaching.

"Hi Will," Georgy replied. "Getting your exercise again, right?"

"You bet," Will said. "I have to do a bit every day, especially if I know that you are coming over. I would not want my exercise getting in the way of our visiting time, Georgy."

"I'll help you with the wood, Will."

"Thank you," Will replied.

Will said they would take off down the trail when they finished stacking the wood. He went inside and brought out his knife.

"All done," Will said.

"Wow," Georgy said, as he saw the leather sheath he had just completed. "Put it on, Will.

"Will tied the leather strings around his leg.

"Is that knife balanced, Will?"

"It sure is, Georgy."

"Did you ever throw knives?"

"I have thrown knives for years. Would you like to learn, Son?"

"Would I ever! I've tried throwing my jackknife, but it would never hit blade first."

"I would have to practice a bit myself, but maybe we can try it when we get back. We can set this piece of board up and practice later on."

As the three of them starting walking down the path, Will waited until they were deep within the forest, and then stepped off the trail. Ben left to amuse himself. Will began by pointing at a huge tree with a large trunk. It was missing a strip of bark.

"This tree is called a Red Cedar. If it remains left alone, it could grow to be well over one hundred and fifty feet tall. It boasts large drooping branches, with scale-like leaves that are

arranged in fan-like sprays. You can smell the strong aroma of these leaves throughout the forest, Georgy. The cones are egg shaped with several pairs of scales. As you can see, the trunk spreads out wide at the base. On mature trees, the bark is grey and stringy and tears off in long strips. You'd find these kinds of trees along the coast in low to mid elevations, where the climate is cool, mild and moist. Georgy, these trees seem to love shade and have sometimes survived over 1,000 years. If you notice, they are surrounded by a lush layer of ferns, huckleberries and Devil's Club. Thick carpets of mosses generally cover the forest floor. The Cedar tree is the cornerstone of the Northwest coast aboriginal culture, with great spiritual significance. The wood is used for dugout canoes, bentwood boxes, clothing, house planks, and tools like arrow shafts, masks and paddles. The inner bark was used to make rope, clothing and baskets. The long arching branches were twisted into rope and baskets. The wood is resistant to decay and insect damage. Fallen tree's wood can remain sound for over 100 years."

Will pointed to another tree nearby, "This is also a Cedar tree, a Yellow Cedar," he said. "Its branches spread out and droop with small, loosely hanging branchlets. Its leaves are bluish-green and slender with sharp points. Unlike the Red Cedar, the leaves of the Yellow Cedar are all alike. The leaf covered twigs appear four-sided rather than flat. The cones are round and berry-like in the first year, becoming woody as they mature."

How tall does this tree grow to be, Will?" Georgy asked inquisitively.

"About half the size of the Red Cedar, around seventy feet tall. The bark on young trees is thin, greyish brown and scaly. On mature trees it has narrow intersecting ridges. The inside of the bark smells like potato skins. You find these trees grow well in deep, moist soil, usually as

single trees or in small clumps. It is common in old growth stands at low elevations with Red Cedar and Western Hemlock, and plants such as Salal and Deer Fern. At high elevations it grows with mountain Hemlock and Fir trees. Like the Red Cedar, aboriginal people along the coast used this wood for paddles, masks, dishes and bows. They wove the bark to make clothing and blankets." "What does a Hemlock and Fir tree look like, Will?"

"A Douglas Fir tree can reach over two hundred feet tall on the coast. Older trees have a long, branch-free trunk. Their leaves are flat needles with a pointed tip. They stand out around the twig. The bark is smooth, grey-brown with gummy resin-filled blisters. It becomes very thick with age, with deeply grooved, dark reddish-brown ridges. Many animals eat Douglas Fir seeds, including squirrels, chipmunks, mice and birds like Winter Wrens and Crossbills. Bears often scrape off the bark on young trees and eat the sap layer beneath."

"Aboriginal people in the south part of the province used the wood and boughs as fuel for pit cooking. They also used it for fishing hooks and handles. The boughs were frequently used for covering the floors of lodges and sweat lodges."

"The Western Hemlock is another large tree that can grow to one-hundred and fifty feet in height. It has down-sweeping branches with flat needles for leaves. The bark is dark brown to reddish-brown and becomes thick and strongly grooved with age. The Western Hemlock likes shade and grows abundantly underneath mature trees where they provide an important source of food for Deer and Elk. Coastal people carved this wood because it worked easily into giant feast dishes, spoons, combs, roasting spits and other implements. Some tribes scraped off the inner bark in spring and baked it into cakes. Those are the four main trees that you will commonly find around here, Georgy."

"What about the tree up on the mountain on the edge, Will?"

"Well, oddly enough, that is a Red Cedar tree. It is totally out of place up there. It is the only one of its kind up there. That is what makes it so unique."

"The trees have provided people with many uses, Georgy, but they depend on their relationships with the surrounding environment: that being the soil, air, water and plants. Plants take energy from the sun and provide food and shelter for animals. In turn, many plants need the help of animals to reproduce. Animals eat seeds and spread them, undigested, to surrounding areas. They also spread seeds by picking them up on their feathers and fur. All of the parts work together to provide a healthy, functioning ecosystem. Anyway, Son, that is mainly your mix of trees and plants that make up the dense forests around here. Did you learn something, Georgy?"

"I didn't know these trees played such an important part in the world."

"They are in constant danger of being cut down and logged off. Come Georgy; let's walk back to my cabin. Ben has had quite a good time running around investigating every little thing."

"Come on, boy!" Georgy yelled. Ben was rustling around some bushes, just off the path. He came charging out with a stick in his mouth, wanting to play. Georgy played a little fetch with Ben on their way back to Will's. Will asked Georgy to sit at the wooden table outside. He fastened Ben to the rope, and then went inside to bring out his knife.

"Could you get us some water, Georgy?" Will asked. "There are some cups just inside the door on the counter." Georgy dipped the ladle into the barrel and filled the cups. He poured some into a pot that was outside so Ben could have a drink, too. Will came out with the knife still in its sheath. He also brought another one that was about the same size, but older, as the wooden handle was worn. The blade was still shiny though. Will took a drink of water and looked over at the piece of board he had set up before they left for the path.

Will went over to it and set it head height onto a tree. He hammered a nail into it to keep it steady, and then backed away as if to study it. He stood about twenty feet back and then threw the knife. It whizzed through the air, striking the board blade first.

"Wow!" Georgy said." Good shot, Will. That knife is really stuck in there."

"It kind of surprised me too, Georgy. It has been a number of years since I've thrown a knife."

"Are you going to throw your new one, Will?"

"No, I would rather not risk putting a dent or scratches on it, Georgy. Once you are confident in throwing a knife, it doesn't matter which one you throw. It just has to be a good knife. My new one won't get too worn out this way either. Would you like to try, Georgy?"

"I'd love to," Georgy replied.

Will pulled the knife out from the target. Taking five steps back, he asked Georgy to come to that spot. He handed Georgy the knife.

"Now take aim," Will said.

Georgy took the knife by the blade and held it up by his shoulder.

"Not like that," Will said. "Hold it by the handle. The knife weighs the same on both ends. You won't cut yourself this way."

Georgy turned the knife around then again took aim. He threw the knife toward the target, but missed, hitting the tree three feet below the mark, bouncing the knife off in the other direction.

"You see what could happen if that was my new knife?"

"This is harder than it looks, Will."

"It takes practice, Georgy."

Georgy tried it a few more times, hitting blade first once, but the knife fell out onto the ground.

"The more you try the easier it will become. Would you like to practice for a little while?"

"No, I'd better get going, Will. Thanks for everything you taught me today. You sure are a smart man."

"Are the kids still giving you a hard time at school?" Will asked.

"Jason Miller said sorry, but some other kids are still being mean. Jason started it, too."

With that, Will let Ben off the rope. Georgy said goodbye to Will and started off down the trail.

"I'll wait for you by your barn at four in the morning, Georgy. Make sure you get up and are out there on time. I will bring the gear."

"Okay, Will," Georgy replied. "How will you know where you're going in the dark?"

"I might bring a torch, but somehow I think the moon will help me."

"Okay, Will, I'll see your tomorrow," Georgy said confidently.

When Georgy got home he couldn't stop talking about what he learned about the trees.

"You sure are learning a lot from Will," Georgy's Mum said.

"Yup. We're going fishing tomorrow morning. Can you wake me up really, really early tomorrow, Mum?"

"How early?"

"I have to meet Will by four o'clock at the barn."

"That is very early, Georgy. You' better get to bed early tonight. This better not interfere with us going to church tomorrow."

"No Mum, that's why we're going so early, because that's when you catch the fish, right Dad?" "Will knows best. I am sure that is why he was there so early each day to fish. He always had a couple when he was done."

Georgy went to bed shortly after dinner. There was a full moon, so they'd have some light to see where they were going. Georgy's Mum got his clothes together and fixed a bag of baked goodies and a canteen of water for them. Ben wouldn't be allowed to go, so he had to sleep inside the house, otherwise he would cause a fuss and follow them.

The next morning, Georgy awoke to his mother gently moving him.

"It is twenty minutes to four, Son. Get dressed and wash your face. I have made you some oatmeal downstairs."

Georgy got up and looked out his window. It wasn't that dark out thanks to the full moon. He could see the chicken coop in the moonlight. Just then he remembered Will would be waiting for him. Georgy quickly dressed and scooted into the bathroom to wash. A few minutes later it was time to go. Georgy grabbed his bag of goodies and bundled himself up into a warm coat. Ben whined as Georgy looked out the door for Will.

"Hello Georgy," Will called out from the barn. "You're right on time."

Georgy said good morning to Will as he left the house.

"I've got some food for us to eat," Georgy said.

"I have a net, a couple of rods for us to use and I have rustled up some worms from under a log by my cabin yesterday after you had left," Will replied.

"How far down is the river, Will?"

"It is only a short distance from here. It will only take us about fifteen minutes to get there."

The moonlight helped lead their way through the trees in the forest. Will walked fast. Georgy

had to skip along to keep up the pace.

"I'm glad you know where you're going, Will. I'd be lost right about now."

"I have travelled this trail hundreds of times in the dark. Once your eyes get used to it, it's easy."

When they got to the river, Georgy tried to imagine his Dad and Mr. Miller hiding behind a tree watching Will fish.

"We are going to go over to a rock ledge. Watch your step."

The last part of the trail led them down to the river bank and onto a rock ledge. There was a mist on the top of the water. The river was rushing by and sounded like it was all around them. They were standing about five feet above the water. It was a good spot to fish from. Will cautioned Georgy about talking out loud.

"If you talk over the sound of the river you will be shouting, and the fish will hear you."

Will baited the two rods and handed one to Georgy. Together they began to fish. It took only a few minutes before Will felt a tug on his line.

"You see, Georgy, they are hungry this morning," Will whispered hoarsely.

Just then Georgy felt a tug on his line.

"I got one, Will!" he said.

"Shhh," Will whispered loudly. "Reel it in, Boy."

Will netted his fish, then Georgy's.

"This is great, Will," Georgy said.

By now day break had given a dusk-like appearance to the late night's darkness. It was so peaceful being down there. Georgy could see the white bone pieces on the handle of the hunting knife that Will brought with him.

"Are we going to clean the fish, Will?"

"Yes, Georgy, but not before we get a few more."

By the time 7am had come around, Georgy and Will had caught themselves a total of six fish. The sun was shining and the mist had disappeared. Georgy shared his food with Will. Finally, they could talk normally.

"Will, you said you had climbed that mountain with the tree on the edge many times. Did you go there to get away?"

"Georgy, there are magical things that happen up on the ledge. They only happen to certain special people that have proven their trust and loyalty to everything around them up there. If you believe with all your heart that you will never hurt the trees or animals or threaten them in any way, you will see what I mean."

"What will I see?"

"That is not for me to say, but most people that have tried to climb up to the top never make it. They get angry at not being able to get there and end up going back down."

"Why can't they reach the top, Will?"

"I believe it is just a lack of patience and desire."

"Will you take me up there someday, Will?"

"Not so soon, Georgy. It is something that you must do on your own when you are a little older and stronger." "Braveheart was my age, Will," Georgy pleaded.

"Yes, but Braveheart lived with the birds, animals and trees in his heart his whole life. Don't worry, Georgy, if you are determined enough, you will get there. Now, let's clean these fish."

Will showed Georgy how to clean the fish. It took Will no time at all. His knife was so sharp.

"Now you do the last one, Georgy."

Will carefully guided Georgy through the lesson and said, "Pretty easy, isn't it?"

"Yeah. You just have to be careful with the bones," Georgy said.

Will threw the waste back into the river, and then took Georgy down to the water's edge to wash up.

"We better get you home, Georgy. It is about 7:30. I don't want your mother worrying."

Just as they were about to leave, an Eagle swooped down and plucked an unsuspecting fish out of the river. "You see, Georgy, just like when Braveheart and his Grandfather fished. The Eagle sits and waits for the right moment to dive."

Eight
A Rain Stick for Some Memories

Georgy and Will walked back up the trail to Georgy's where they saw his Dad feeding the horse. "Dad, we caught six fish, three each. It was perfect," Georgy said with excitement.

Ben heard them and came bolting over, sniffing at the fish.

"Good morning to you both," Dad said. "You have already cleaned them, I see."

"Your son learned to clean his fish this morning," Will said. "He did it well."

"That's because I used Will's knife, Dad. Look at what he made."

Georgy's Dad came over and shook Will's hand. Will pulled the knife out of its sheath and handed it to him.

"That's pretty impressive, Will. It's got a good sturdy feel to it and it's balanced. This is the kind of knife one could throw."

"Will doesn't want to get scratches on it. He showed me how to throw a different knife yesterday. Will threw it and stuck it right into the target!"

"Don't forget, Georgy, I've had a couple of years to practice."

"Well, you'd better get going on your chores, Georgy. I hear some pretty hungry chickens over there," Georgy's Dad said. "Then you'd better settle down for a nap before church. You were up really early this morning."

"Here, Georgy, take your fish," Will said.

"Thanks for taking me fishing, Will. Maybe we'll see you later, if I'm not too tired."

Will coughs a few times. "I guess I'm catching something. It's probably just a little cold. Have a good day, Georgy, and thanks for being on time."

"Goodbye, Will," Georgy's Dad said, "And thank you for all that you've done for my son. He just loves every minute he spends with you."

"He is good company and shows a willingness to learn. He is a good boy, Mr. Walker."

Will turned and set off towards the trail home. Georgy did his chores and then laid down for a little rest. Ben jumped up beside Georgy on his bed.

"You missed me, didn't you, boy." Georgy said. Together they rested until Georgy fell asleep.

A couple of weeks passed. Georgy periodically checked in on Will, only to find his cough had gotten worse instead of better. Georgy was really worried because the day came when he and his Dad had to deliver groceries to Will again. Georgy had been knocking, but Will wasn't answering. Georgy went around back to where Will was usually cutting wood and found him lying there on top of the wood cuttings.

"Dad! Come quick!" Georgy called.

His Dad found Will to be totally exhausted.

"He's not been well, Dad. I guess he tried to cut wood but was too sick to chop it. He's been like this ever since we went fishing a few weeks ago."

Georgy's Dad woke Will up and helped him into the cabin and onto a cot. Georgy gave Will some water then brought some wood inside as his Dad lit a fire and put the groceries away.

Hello Georgy," Will said. "I guess I was a little tired."

"You have so much wood outside on the pile already. What are you doing chopping more when you're sick?" "I'm just trying to beat this flu. You have to keep going, you know. I have to get my exercise, Boy."

"I'll get you more water, Will."

"Can we make you something?" Georgy's Dad asked.

"No thank you. I'll be okay now. Thanks for bringing my groceries over to me again and thanks for caring to help me in this situation."

"You let Georgy know if you need help with wood, Will."

"Can I stay for a bit, Dad?"

"What do you say, Will?" his Dad asked.

"I would love the company."

"I'll see you at home, Son."

"First, we have to attach Ben to his rope outside, Dad." After his Dad left, Will asked Georgy,

"What day is your birthday?"

"It's today, Will. I'm ten years old today, just like Braveheart."

"I have something for you, Georgy. Look behind the closet door."

Georgy opened the door and found a large rain stick leaning against the wall."

"Is this for me, Will?" Georgy asked excitedly.

"I couldn't think of anybody else I would rather see have it," Will answered.

"Thanks so much, Will. I absolutely love this rain stick." Georgy closed his eyes and turned it upside down. Hundreds of hard pieces of grain trickled down through dozens of tiny wooden rod pieces, creating the sound of rain falling all around.

"Are you sure you're going to be okay, Will?" Georgy asked.

"I am just a little tired and weak from being outside."

"I'll heat up the soup on the stove, Will." Georgy did just that then took a bowl over to Will.

"Thank you, Georgy," Will said, as he sipped the hot soup.

Georgy played with his rain stick. When Will was finished eating he lay his head down on his pillow and shut his eyes.

"I guess I better go now, Will. You get some rest and I'll check on you tomorrow."

"Thanks, Georgy. I hope you have had a wonderful birthday."

"I have now. Thanks for my present."

Georgy saw himself out. He showed Ben the rain stick. When he turned it upside down, Ben cocked his head to one side and sniffed at it. Georgy unhooked him from the rope and together they walked back home. Georgy couldn't wait to show his folks the rain stick. He decided to take it to school to show everyone.

The same kids continued to ridicule him when they learned who had given him the gift, but Georgy didn't care any longer. He went straight to Will's after school.

Nine
Wildheart

When Georgy knocked on the door, nobody answered. He knocked again, and then went inside. Will looked horrible. He was very weak and pale. The fire in the stove had gone out and the house was cold.

"Georgy, please get me some water," Will whispered.

Georgy ran outside and hurriedly dipped a cup from the barrel.

"Come here," Will said weakly.

"No Will, I've got to go get my Dad. He'll get you a doctor."

"Georgy, I've got to tell you something."

"What is it Will?" Georgy asked in a scared voice.

"You remember Braveheart and his Grandfather?"

"Of course, Will. What about them?"

"That little boy Braveheart was me."

"You're Braveheart?" Georgy asked as tears began to swell in his eyes. "Yes, and you have been my best friend since we first met. Son, you really have a good heart. You have been a good listener, and have such an inquisitive mind. I have a name for you. I have never felt this sick and I was a little afraid, so I engraved the name on something I would like you to have."

"What is the name, Will?"

"Wildheart, Son," Will replied, then coughed in pain. "Look under my pillow."

Georgy lifted the pillow and found the hunting knife that Will had recently made.

"Oh no. You don't mean it, do you, Will?" Georgy asked worriedly.

"Look on the handle."

Georgy noticed Will had carved the nine letters down one side of the bone piece on the front of the handle.

"Will, you are going to be okay. I need to go get my Dad."

Georgy ran out of the cabin and all the way home. He returned with his Dad, who quickly lit a

fire to boil some water.

"Georgy, you stay with Will and wipe down his forehead with a damp cloth. I will go get the doctor." When his Dad drove off, Will looked at Georgy with eyes half open.

"Wildheart, do you like your gift?" "I love it, Will. Thank you so much. I will never lose it and will learn to throw it, just like you do." "Remember the mountain, Wildheart. The magical mountain."

By the time Georgy's Dad returned with the doctor Will had fallen into a deep sleep. The doctor had quite a time trying to wake him. Georgy sat at the end of the cot and quietly cried, scared that Will was going to die. Georgy's Dad put his hand on his son's shoulder and comforted him.

"What does it look like, Doctor?" Georgy's Dad asked.

"He has Pneumonia. I wouldn't bank on him lasting the night. Can you get someone from the

village to stay with him for a few hours?"

"We will stay," Georgy's Dad said.

The doctor took Will's pulse again, but this time he couldn't find one.

"I'm afraid he's gone. You had best let the people in his Band know."

"Georgy, I'm sorry," his Father said.

Georgy began to sob. "He can't die, Dad. He's got so much he wants to show me. How can he die now?" "I'm sorry, Son," the doctor said as he pulled the sheet over Will's head.

"He gave me this, Dad," Georgy cried as he showed his Dad the knife. "He gave me a name and carved it on the handle. Look."

Georgy's Dad read it. "Wildheart. Will was really proud of you, Son, and I knew he taught

a lot of values as he told you those stories."

"He said I was his best friend," Georgy sobbed.

"Let's go, Son. We've got to tell the others."

They told the village folk on the Reservation and asked to be told when Will would be buried, as they would need to be there at his funeral; then they left for home. Georgy stared quietly at his knife all the way home.

The funeral was the following week. Georgy, his Dad, Mr. Miller and Jason came to pay their final respects. The whole time Georgy sat stone faced. He didn't say a word. Finally, he turned to his Dad and said, "I want to climb up that mountain, the one with the big Red Cedar on the

ledge."

"It's too dangerous," his Dad said on the way home.

"When won't it be dangerous, Dad?" Georgy asked angrily. "Braveheart did it when he was ten!" "He grew up in the forest, Son. There's a big difference there."

Georgy told his Dad all about Braveheart and his Grandfather.

"Do you know who Braveheart was Dad?"

"Was it Will, Son?"

"You bet. I am never going to forget him."

Life for Georgy Walker changed on that day. He still played with Ben in the clover field, but at school he kept to himself. He got his Dad to put a piece of board up on the side of the barn so he could practice throwing his knife. In time he got to be pretty good at it, even though he was only standing ten feet back from the target. At least it was sticking in blade first. Not bad for a ten-year-old.

Soon school was out for the summer and Georgy felt like a free man. The kids had quit bugging him around the time Will had died, so he was back on speaking terms with everybody. Georgy thought of Will. He would have spent his entire summer at Will's house if he were still alive.

He still had Jason, but Jason's Dad would have him working every day in the store. That left Ben. He actually made for good company. He had never let Georgy down before either.

One hot summer day Georgy filled a canteen with water and took Ben to their favourite playground. They played fetch and ended up wrestling around amongst the warm field of clover. Ben would never stop. He loved to play. Georgy's Dad let him hang around with him while Georgy was at school, but all he did was roam and investigate the area around him. It was when Georgy took him to the field that he could really cut loose.

Georgy also knew that after a while Ben would settle down and have a little dog snooze. That's the time that Georgy would use to gaze up high into the sky and begin his favourite pastime, daydreaming.

PART II
The Dream

Ten
Georgy's Dream

"Ben, that's enough. I'm exhausted. It's got to be over eighty degrees out here in the sun."

Georgy found a little shade beside a small patch of bush.

"Come here, boy, and have some water. Let's rest for a bit."

Georgy opened a canteen, poured water into his hat and offered it to Ben who eagerly lapped it up. He and Ben stretched out along side each other. A soft, cool breeze began to fan across Georgy's face. He stared up at the nearby mountain. He wondered how old the tree must be, and what it would be like to be up there poking his head through the satin white clouds that silently hovered above the big ledge on the front side, facing him. Georgy felt his eyelids getting heavy. It wasn't too long before Georgy fell into a deep, deep sleep.

(In his dream, Georgy is a father telling a story to his son, Taylor.)

"You see it, Son? That big, black thing flying around the clouds? Look, there's a smaller black speck flying beside it. That's the eagle teaching his little one to fly. It must be so much fun being able to dive in and out of the clouds like that."

"Dad, that's the eagle that perches on the totem pole up on the ledge, isn't it? You said when I was older you'd tell me the story of how that totem got to be there."

"You're right, Son. Once upon a time there was a young boy, about 10 years old. That young boy was me."

For a young boy, living out here in the country meant you had lots of free time to entertain yourself as you pleased. The down side was that there weren't too many neighbours to share the free time with. Our nearest neighbours lived miles away and we only went to town on Saturday.

So for me, a typical summer consisted of playing fetch with my dog in a field and visiting with an old native man, Will Williams, who lived alone in a cabin out in the woods, within the Reserve. I liked going to see him because he told me stories of a young native boy and his Grandfather and about his life when he was young, playing on the mountain. He called me Wildheart. Will said the name suited me. He told me he was a Chief. I never saw anyone else ever visit him. I remember sitting so quietly, my eyes fixed on him, not wanting to miss a single word. Those visits seemed to last for hours.

I also remember leaving to go back home. I'd think about the story he had just told me. Sometimes I'd pretend I was a cowboy and I'd gallop my way back home. Then I'd just walk for a while and kick the leaves off the dirt and moss covered pathway in front of me. I enjoyed doing that all summer long.

One fall day, after hearing about how the Indians communicated by sending smoke signals, I thought I would show Will that I could do it, too. One afternoon as Will fell asleep I took some wooden matches that were sitting on the table. He had said that nobody should try this because it was dangerous and that the only ones who knew how to do it were the natives.

Anyway, I left, intending only to start a small fire. A short distance from Will's cabin, I found some dry twigs beneath the heavy branches of a Cedar and lit them. It had started to sprinkle but the branches sheltered the lit matches from the wind and rain.

In no time I had a small fire going. The problem was it didn't stay in one spot. I tried to put it out but couldn't. Just as I was about to run back to get Will, he rushed by me with a blanket and snuffed out the fire. He scolded me and said I was lucky he had smelled the smoke. He said that in another few minutes the whole forest might have been on fire. I felt pretty bad. I had singed branches and burned some bushes. Worst of all, I had made Will mad.

He said he wasn't angry but I knew he was. At that point he looked at me and said, "Wildheart, from now on this is the name I will call you." He said he appreciated my company and that no other kids ever cared to come by and visit with him.

We got to be very good friends. He taught me about life. He taught me a lot about the trees in the forest. I could name all the different trees by the age of ten. Will could tell what was wrong with them just by looking at the bark. He said he used to study trees as a child. He seemed to know everything about them.

I used to really worry about him, though. He said he'd gotten used to people not bothering him, but he seemed so lonely. I would have spent all day with him if I could have, but he said it would be best if I came in the afternoon, unless we were going fishing. Some days he was up early carving and he was too busy for me to visit him, so I stayed away for most of the day. Saturdays after my chores were done, when we'd get back from town, I had the rest of the day to myself. I'd take my dog out to the field where we'd wrestle and play fetch for hours. After that we'd lie down and watch the shapes of the clouds pass by overhead. It was so relaxing to lay there and daydream. My gaze would often turn to a nearby mountain where the clouds almost always skimmed over.

You see, I was never allowed to go up the mountain because of the steep cliffs and rocky terrain. I wanted only to be able to someday, be grown up enough to climb right up to the very top so that I could reach out and touch those clouds. In that way I, too, could feel a part in the peacefulness that they seemed to possess.

For years I had watched an eagle circle high above a single Red Cedar tree near a cliff at the top of the mountain. I had no idea that over the years, both the eagle and the tree, who I had watched, had also been very aware of my activities down here.

Anyway, I had to be happy being a small boy with big dreams. I hoped that someday I would grow up to be a forest ranger. Then I could climb up any mountain any time I wanted to.

Summer seemed to stay around forever, but before long, there wasn't a leaf to be seen on any of the trees. One day, I decided to go to s Will's cabin, hoping to catch another story. I noticed there was no smoke coming out from the small pipe in the roof, indicating he was not using his wood stove. I wondered if he was even home. He rarely left the cabin except to get wood from out back. I decided to knock. It was cold outside. I just wanted to be sure he was all right. To my surprise he answered my knock by meekly calling out my name. I opened the door and looked in.

He was lying in his cot, sick as I'd ever seen him. I thought maybe he'd caught a bad cold but he could hardly lift his head off the pillow. I quickly got him some water, and noticed his eyes were only half open. I lit a lantern and fired up the woodstove. It was so cold in there. Will just lay there barely moving. I had to run home to get my dad to come help him.

I still remember the way he spoke to me. He was short of breath and very weak. My childhood memories revolved around the old man. What I am today is a result of the time he gave to me. It made me so sad to look at him lying there so helpless.

I recall being teased by my friends in town. Jason Miller was the worst. He was one of my school mates. His Dad owned the general store. Mr. Miller was nice. He would drive some supplies out to Will once a month. Jason used to go with him and make up lies and stories about him. Jason would say, "That guy's weird. He looks mean. I know if my Dad wasn't with me, he'd capture me and keep me tied up like a prisoner. He told me to keep away from him." Jason's Dad would say, "Now, Jason, Will is harmless. He is just old and doesn't have many people he can talk with." I would agree and tell them Will was the smartest, kindest person I had ever met. He wouldn't hurt a fly. Jason thought the old man was crazy and he thought I was crazy to waste my time on him. Because of Jason, everyone in town teased me.

Anyway, Will passed away that same day. Just before he died, he gave me the name Wildheart and asked that I remember the mountain. As a young boy, he too, had dreamed of climbing to the top and touching the clouds. The difference was, he did just that. He said, "Wildheart, you have patiently listened to the stories I have told you. You must never let them disappear. The art of storytelling has become a frittered away and forgotten tradition." He told me that if he had to do it all over again, he would live up there, that it was a magical place where one's imagination was free to run wild; a place to get away from it all.

Funny, though, he never went into any detail about actually being there. He did, however, say that he listened to the storytelling of the Elders and that he would sit spellbound for hours, captivated by the visions they would bring. It sounds to me like he wasn't the only one up there.

I asked him why he chose to teach me. I felt kind of special. He said someday I would find out for myself. All I knew was that he loved the mountain and that it had served as a sanctuary to him for a long, long time. Many years went by. I grew up fast. I graduated from high school and entered university. I studied Forestry and Conservation, but I never forgot about the mountain, or Will.

Eleven
Climbing the Mountain

One summer, many years later, I returned home from university. I decided to hike up that mysterious mountain. Thinking back to my first urge for going, I pressed onward toward the top. For the most part the climb was easy going. Light brush and the odd dead tree to stumble over were to be expected. I stayed well away from the edge and found that it wasn't as steep as I originally figured. Of course, I was a little older and bigger, too.

About one hundred feet from the top I found a long, wide trench filled with thick brush, making it difficult for anyone to go any further. There were steep slopes on either side, so I'd have to go through it to get up to the top.

I decided I should return home to get some tools. After all these years I wasn't about to let a stupid barricade ruin my chance to get to the top of this mountain.

Before leaving I heard a thrashing noise across the bushes. I couldn't see what was causing it, so I hid and threw some stones in that direction, hoping to get its attention. It worked, but to my horror a big old black bear stood up and sniffed the air.

"Did you run, Dad, or were you too scared?" asked Taylor.

"I stayed put, Son," replied Georgy. "He was on the other side of the barricade and couldn't get to me, so I knew I was safe." I waited a couple of minutes until the bear settled down, then quietly left for home.

I returned the following day with an axe and a machete. I let my dog come along this time, just in case the bear was still in the area. As we got closer to the barricade I heard some shots. I heard some kids yell, "I got him! He fell into the bushes!"

As we approached, three kids in their teens were target practicing with a small rifle. Were they ever shocked to see me. I asked the one with the gun what he had shot. He said he just shot a pheasant, but it had fallen into the brush and they couldn't get to him.

I didn't know who the kids were. I had never seen them before. I told them I had work to do and that they should leave. Grudgingly they agreed and left.

I began hacking a path through the thick brush. My dog was having a great time sniffing around and getting into every little thing. A couple of hours into my job I heard a faint rustling sound coming from a few yards from where I was working. I could make out the feathers of a wing as it started flapping. It took me a few minutes to get over to it. There I found an injured eagle. It frantically flapped around screeching at me. This is what those kids shot. I was so angry that they could be so cruel. I had to save the poor bird, but he'd snap at me if I got too close to him.

I threw my jacket over him then scooped him up with my gloves. I had to hold him tight and in close to my body or he'd fight his way free. Getting down the mountain without using my arms was tricky. My dog could sense the eagle inside my jacket and was driving me nuts trying to jump up to get a sniff at it. I hoped my tools would be safe there. I had visions of those kids returning to get the eagle and then stealing them.

Anyhow, Son, we got home ok. I took the eagle to the vet. After the bird was sedated, I told the Vet I would like to care for him at my house. I put the bird in my dog's old travel kennel until I could make him a cage out of chicken wire and wood.

The bird was tuckered out for a few days. With the Vet's help I was able to sponge bathe and bandage him up with no trouble. He didn't even open his eyes. Luckily the bullet had only grazed him, but he had bled quite a bit.

I fed and nursed him back to health. I kept this up for about three straight weeks while working on the mountain every day. By the way, those kids never came back and I found my tools right where I had left them.

Meanwhile, the eagle seemed well enough for me to consider letting him go. His diet had been mainly toast, water and scrambled eggs, although he seemed to like any food scraps I'd throw into his cage. One Sunday my dog and I went fishing in a nearby creek. We were lucky enough to catch a couple of trout.

Son, that was the last meal we fed to the eagle before setting him free. My dog had gotten used to having the bird around even if he hadn't been too friendly. I knew he needed to get back into the wild. I lifted his cage up from the table and took it outside.

I had built the cage big enough so that when I took off his bandages he could use the bad wing to flap around and learn how to use it again. A funny thing happened when I opened his cage to let him go. He just stood there, like he wasn't sure what he should do. He let me reach in and lift him out without a struggle. It was as if he didn't want to go.

My dog fixed that in a hurry. He was so excited to finally see the bird outside his cage that he came running over to get a really good sniff. That was enough to send the eagle into orbit. His wings flapped like nothing had ever happened. Up he went towards the mountain he called home.

I was sad to see him go, but happy that I had saved him and could make him well enough to get on with his life in his natural surroundings.

The next day I set out to finish what I'd started on the mountain. I had already made a good enough path through the brush. It wouldn't take long to complete. Then I'd have no trouble making it the rest of the way up. That barricade had been at least thirty feet long.

It ended up taking a couple of hours to finish clearing a half decent pathway through the

Twelve
Meeting Tree

In a clearing stood a single Cedar tree with a perfectly round hole through one of its bottom branches. Moving closer I found the tree to be out on a ledge by the side of a cliff. All at once a thunderous voice bellowed, "Stay away from the ledge!"

Startled and confused, I drew closer to the tree. A weird sensation came over me. It felt like something was nudging me to look through the hole in the branch. Once I did, I began to question my state of mind because what I saw was a different kind of place, nothing like I was accustomed to seeing before.

Through the opening I saw green grass in the valley below and tall trees touching the blue sky with their outstretched might. Wild animals in abundance, and birds singing, dipping playfully in the fresh air. I could "hear" whisper-like goodbyes from the early morning dew as it suddenly evaporated from the leaves as the rays of sunshine began to push down through the heavy tree arms. This truly was a magical setting, for what I saw wasn't visible anywhere else but through the hole in the branch.

I stood frozen against that looking glass in time. As I turned to leave, the voice boomed again. "Stay away from the ledge!"

This time it came from within the tree. I wondered if this might be some sort of scare tactic. Suddenly I began to think that I might not be welcome there on the ledge. But who was doing the talking? Trees can't talk.

I had never been a threat to anyone or anything before. I decided to move over to the edge to take a look down below. I saw the clover fields and was surprised to find that this was the very tree, so high up on the cliff that I had gazed at for so many years. If it weren't for such a clear day, the clouds would probably be hovering above this very tree. It was such an experience. Just how I thought it might be.

I scurried back to the branch to contemplate my next move. As I looked closely at the tree, I noticed two hollowed out knotholes that looked as though they could be eyes. This tree was more than alive. It was unusually human-like.

What I had seen through the hole in the branch made me think about how our earth was supposed to look, yet it was so different now. It made me think of the future. I felt a little confused at what I had just seen, yet I understood and couldn't help feeling partly responsible. "You probably didn't want me to see how beautiful our world really was for fear I'd take it for granted even more, am I right, Tree?" Then the tree spoke, "Your friend Will who passed away loved life. He believed in his heart that someday this could be a place for all to come and admire Mother Earth's beauty; to some day be able to look around and see what you saw through the hole in my branch. That was Will's passion."

"He chose you to share in his life. You learned the traditions as a young boy because he trusted you. You have always been a good listener with keen interests and an ability to learn quickly. You showed him that you also felt the need for change to a higher standard of living. Your feelings for what you've seen here are no different from Will's."

"He knew that it would take a very special person to bridge the gap between the careless and caring in their past and present state of affairs. If we were to lose interest in restoring our planet, we would risk ruining life itself for future generations to come. He was a caring man."

"What is your name?" Tree asked.

"Georgy Walker," he replied.

"Look high into my branches. Can you see him?" Tree asked.

"Yes, it's an Eagle. He looks like the wounded bird I found on the mountain. Why does he stare?" "He trusts few," Tree said. Eagle is concerned at losing the forest of tall trees down below. I am all that is left for an him to nest in because I have managed to scare everything else away from getting too close to me. It's been well over fifty years since the barricade on mountainside has let anyone through. Not one person has set foot up here but then nobody has shown the desire or determination either."

At that moment Eagle pushed off the branch and gracefully glided within feet of where Georgy was sitting. Georgy recognized the large bird.

"You were eagle that I rescued from near death. You never came back. You didn't seem to b every thankful," Georgy said.

"You people abuse your gun privileges," Eagle said. "How was I supposed to know you weren't part of that group of people shooting at anything and everything that moved on the mountain? I was trying to scare them away from here. There is one thing I know, A bear would surely have gotten to me before too long if you hadn't found me."

"You won't have to worry about the bear anymore," Georgy said. "A hunter shot and killed him yesterday down the other side of the mountain."

"I do thank you for helping save my life. Since that time, Tree has taught me about revenge. Revenge is like a double-edged sword. It destroys the enemy and one's soul. It forces us to live like shadows in a wounded heart. Somehow though, the good people seem to be attracted to this window in the world. Maybe, together we might uplift the souls of many."

Suddenly, Eagle launched off the branch and soared down to the valley below.

"You know, nothing good or very bad lasts long," Tree said. "Eagle was hard to convince of this as a younger bird. You must go now, Georgy, but come back to the ledge in seven days."

Georgy said goodbye. A lot went through his mind as he wound his way down the mountain side toward home. For seven straight days he thought a lot about the job at hand. He was but one man and it was like there was an entire world to teach out there.

Thirteen

Memories of an Old Man

A week later, as Georgy ascended the mountain again, he could feel the presence of something very close to him. Finally, Georgy turned quickly to see a large black Raven dive out of sight behind some branches.

"Come here," Georgy beckoned. "Let's have a look at you."

The Raven swooped over to a branch just above Georgy's head. Cocking his head sideways, he said, "So you're the one everyone has been talking about. I hope you know what you're getting yourself into. I could care less about what happens around here, just as long as I can keep picking at the garbage people throw out every day off the pathway. You'll soon get tired of that tree telling you to go and come back every seven days. I think he's testing you."

Georgy was not amused. He thought of tossing a rock at the bird but thought of Tree. The way Tree spoke so caringly had begun to impact him. To help yourself use your hand, but to help others use your heart. Besides, Raven was only teasing him. He obviously had nothing better to do than pester someone.

"Remember not so long ago when forests were in no danger of being logged?" Georgy asked. "And of a time when hikers and campers respected the land and the wildlife that so dearly relied on the consistent well-being of those forests, so their young could be born and flourish, unharmed in their natural habitat?"

"Well, that was then, old boy," Raven replied. "You are starting to sound like Eagle up on the ledge. Good-bye. I really must go investigate the rest of this mountainside." Raven flapped his wings and flew off.

Georgy had to remind himself that not everybody was going to have this kind of outlook in life and as far as the Tree testing him, well, Georgy was only too happy to accept the invitation to return to the mountain anytime he was asked. So, with a shake of his head, Georgy shrugged it off and resumed his climb to the top of the mountain.

When he got there, Georgy approached Tree and immediately found himself involved in conversation.

"Think about the old man who used to tell you stories. That poor old man with grey hair and hollow cheeks who lived on the edge of the forest. I knew all along that you played in the woods and would call for him just outside his cabin. It was you that would knock at his door patiently awaiting his answer. And it was you who listened and watched with excited eyes as he would share whatever story that happened to be on the tip of his tongue. That was a long time ago. As you grew older, when others had no interest in hearing you talk about him anymore, you still went back, even when other kids laughed and made jokes about him. They would say he was just old and no good for anything. They teased you because you cared for him. You cared until the day he died.

"Georgy," Tree continued, "You were the reason the old man lived. You were a good listener. You were Wildheart. Your younger life revolved around that old man. The images were shallow but your dreams were large. He taught you to be aware of what you believed in, but to let your thoughts run wild. He was the cause of your happiness all those years, just as you were the cause of his. He watched you grow to appreciate life, just as he had."

"How can you be sure of this?" Georgy asked.

"I had a young brave come and sit beneath my branches a very long time ago," Tree said. "He came here to listen to the stories of the Elders, for this too, was their meeting place. This ledge was the safest place as well as the closest place they could get to their Spirit Elders. Enough said for now. You must go now Georgy, but come back in seven days, then we will summon the Spirit Elders."

Georgy never argued at having to leave but was certainly confused by it. Maybe Tree wanted to make sure Georgy was genuinely interested by seeing if he would make the effort to return. Anyway, Georgy said good-bye and headed for home. He wondered what summoning the Spirit Elders was going to entail and what his involvement would be. He was willing to find out.

Georgy felt proud hearing what Will had thought of him. He respected the wisdom the old man possessed. He realized that there could be no wise young men, that it would take a lifetime of learning to even get close to becoming as smart as the old man.

"What have I gotten myself into?" Georgy said aloud. "And what does it all mean? I've found the magic on the mountain. I'm beginning to understand that there is a part of me in those I've met up there. So where do I stand? What do they expect me to do?"

Georgy had a lot to think about before returning to the mountain. He decided to focus on what was important to Will. Obviously a plan would be needed, but Georgy had to be sure of what that plan should entail so he decided to wait until he was back on the ledge to discuss it with Tree.

Fourteen

Back on the Ledge

On the seventh day Eagle intercepted Georgy near the top of the mountain. "I wanted to be sure about you, Georgy, before I could talk comfortably from my heart," Eagle said. "Others have promised to preserve the land only to sell it for hefty profits. They laugh as it slowly becomes torn down."

"The key to our success will be found in the trust we have for each other, Eagle," Georgy stressed. "Besides, have I ever let you down before?"

So it was on that day Georgy and Eagle became good friends. Later, upon reaching the top, Tree, Eagle and Georgy stood together on the ledge high above the valley below.

"We must try to never drift apart," Georgy said. "The world is far more interesting with us three in it together. As I look below, I see our lives surrounded by the landscape which represents Earth's ceremonial paintings."

"Wildheart has finally grown up and come home, Eagle," Tree kidded. It wasn't that long ago that you were of tiny beak and little wings, unable to peer over the high walls of your captive nest. It took an inner courage to get yourself up and over those walls. That struggle will be the same one that faces us with our world today. So, what do you say? Can we make a difference?"

"You bet we can!" Georgy said. "Right, Eagle?"

"I hope so," Eagle replied.

And so together the three friends decided to take on the task of making a difference in the world.

"Georgy, it's time," Tree said. "Tonight you stay here. Together we summon the Spirit Gods. They have not been happy for a long time."

Fifteen
Spirit's Story

(Out on the ledge)

"I wish I had brought a blanket," Georgy shivered. "It gets a bit cool up here at night. Maybe we should sit closer together so we can keep warm."

With that Tree covered Georgy with some heavy branches, keeping him warm.

"I want to tell you a story," Tree said. "There once was a Warlord who was chief among a village of a very proud people. Whenever a troubled brave would call upon him to discuss a problem, he would always leave feeling assured that the Spirits were favourably watching over him. But as time wore on, the chief soon grew very tired and it was not long before they laid him to rest."

"He had taught his people of a love within themselves and how in using it, could glow with a radiance that would please the spirits so high in the sky. They were the storytellers. So sacred were the words of their ancestors. So precious was the voice from within the face behind pretty paint. So vivid were the lines around their eyes. Their image of compassion had no borders. Each of us has been touched with our own childhood memories linking us to our past. We must rekindle those memories in an effort to keep them alive.

"Will told me this just before he died," Georgy said.

It didn't take long before the radiance in the chief's people dimmed as their uncertain future began to grow recklessly out of control. Soon enough, like a compass without direction, the people accepted uncertainty with a still-like gaze.

All of a sudden thunder sounded, as a strong wind blew the swirling clouds apart, creating an opening to the heavens above. It was there that the images of past Chiefs from long ago generations formed and lingered, high above the ledge.

As Georgy stared up at the faces he was both overwhelmed and grateful to be witnessing such a sight. He felt frozen just to stare. Just then a voice came from above, yet no lips moved.

"We have returned to remind you of a time long ago. Back through the dust of many centuries, a dust that represented our people who were scattered and strewn across the land."

The voices sounded like many speaking together in deep monotone sound.

"We represent a most important story. We were the heart and soul of the early West Coast

Tribes. Together we brought peace and love and helped each other in their own way to become one with all elements of nature and its surroundings."

"We were summoned in almost every circumstance of each day in the life of a brave; young or old. During times of uncertainty, we were always there. Time quickly followed. So did the white man and in doing so, squashed the tribal spirit. It didn't start out that way. When the Redskin tribes were many, there were leaders chosen among them. Those leaders were mighty men with no fear. They were picked to guide the warriors in times of battle. The Chief was a proud man whose best interest was in maintaining a happy lifestyle for his people."

"It was necessary to form an army within his people as the white man came to fight with them, slaughtering many and burning down their teepees. The Redskins couldn't understand why those people were coming onto their land. This kept the Redskin hostile. Soon they fought back with a savage vengeance. Yet to so cruelly batter one another could only lead to more bloodshed and hardship." "The chief could not give in to the white man stealing what was theirs, but he saw a greater need to hold on to what was left; To let his people live."

"He called a meeting to bring everyone together. It was time to discuss meeting with the white man in hopes of calling a truce. So at day break the people assembled at the centre of the village. The sun provided the warmth and the sky was blue." "The chief pointed to an eagle gliding in a wide circle high above them."

"He is free. If you want your children's children to live without vengeance in their hearts, you must agree to peace with the white man."

"Word got back to the troops that the Indians wanted to talk about peace. The troop leader sent word back to the Indian settlement that he would agree to meet with the Chief. Through the help of some Indian scouts, they met to begin their talks. And so, after weeks of negotiations, both sides settled on a truce. It wasn't exactly as the Redskin was promised though. Learning houses were built but after some time the Redskins learned that what was once such a great part of their heritage, was frozen still as time passed them by."

"They were not allowed to practice their spiritual rituals. Eventually, the people left or were driven away and their land was taken from them. As you can see, we have been taken advantage of for a very long time. The Redskins have long since been forgotten about. The land, too, has been badly misused and our streams now run muddy. We believe that the only part of the story not yet finished is one of forgiveness, for the Redskin blood that was shed on the battle grounds of old. The environmental massacres that have taken place on land was neither the white man's or the Redskin's."

"To stop the fighting was the best thing both sides could have done for each other," Georgy shouted to the Spirit Elders. "But how can the blame be given to either side? Won't the carelessness of the people toward Earth and the past come back to haunt them?"

"It's you that must be shown," the Spirit Chief said angrily, before you wipe away your own existence. This will be a time to rebuild. A time to change the way you people live."

Sixteen

Fire on the Mountain

Thunder sounded again, as lightning struck at the mountain base below. Gusts of wind spread sparks of fire onto the brush. Slowly the brush fire began to creep up the mountainside.

Below, people began to swarm about, worried that the wind would blow the fire toward their homes. They stood helpless against the threat of lightning striking them. All they could do was watch and pray.

"How can this be allowed to happen?" Georgy asked Tree. "We are promising to change."

"I think that inevitably, all generations are to blame, but it was us that called for the Elders and are right. It must take something like this to get the point across that we all have to show respect for the way in which we treat our planet." Tree replied.

The winds blew in from the north as the fire grew more out of control. Georgy stared helplessly as the fire singed its way up toward the top of the mountain. Tree was in terrible danger. Fire raged in Georgy's mind.

"Where are your Rain Spirits?" Georgy yelled. "Why can't you do something right now?"

Eagle screeched for all he was worth. He refused to leave the branch he was perched on. He watched in dismay as the fire began to climb higher and faster.

As darkness fell, the fire had nearly reached the top of the mountain. Smoke met the swirling thunder clouds high above the blackened earth. The heat was beginning to be unbearable. The only thing keeping Georgy safe was the fact that he was out on the ledge.

One side of Tree's branches began getting singed by the heat. Eagle flew down to the tip of the ledge beside Georgy. Through the opening in the clouds the spirits reappeared. They were still angry.

"We are not happy," the Spirit Chief scolded angrily. "You let your world become destroyed and then you expect Rain Spirits to save you? There must be an example made to show the non-caring that they must stop now. It will be from great sacrifice that you remember this day. There are none so blind as those who will not see."

Georgy was stunned at what that could possibly mean. What he saw was something that would stay with him for the rest of his life.

The sky blackened. Rain began to pour down in torrents. Georgy prayed that the rain would put out the fire as it slickened the mess below. Thunder bellowed as the winds howled. Finally, the wind died down and the fire began to subside. Then, all at once there was a horrific crack sound from lightning with thunder that followed. Lightning lit up the entire sky.

A tremendous bolt of lightning shot down from the heavens and struck Tree. The impact was enough to sheer the top right off altogether, practically killing Tree. It looked as though Tree was barely alive.

"I can't believe what's happening," Georgy shouted to Tree. "Why would the Spirits want to hurt something so dear as you've been? You've stood for everything good in the world. You really cared."

It hurt to look at Tree. So strong had he been. Georgy felt lost at the thought of losing him.

"Tree has taught me more about myself than I could have ever learned on my own," cried Eagle. "He taught me about the world around us."

Sadly, Georgy looked at Tree's wounds.

"My branch with the window to the world has almost been destroyed. The time has come to stop the daydreaming and get on with the reality of saving Earth," Tree said quietly with a shortness of breath.

"You understand, Georgy? It is just like what happened to the Redskin people long ago. Since the first Treaty was signed, they were denied living by their own means. To me this means they were stripped of their dignity. Nobody helped them. This time something is being done about it because it has affected all of mankind. We have no one person to blame but ourselves. We have gradually deprived one another of Mother Earth's greatest offerings. We created this mess out of greed."

"So you see, because Mother Earth suffers, so then must we, as she cries out for vengeance. If these are to be my last words to speak, then be brave and carry on. Do not blame the Spirits for what they have done. You are to carry out this deed, Georgy, for we have all been taught a lesson. I would ask that you remember to use me as a reflection of our heritage."

"I promise you, Tree, that you will live on forever," Georgy said. "I'll transfer you into a beautiful totem pole and set you here for all to see and admire."

"Georgy, please ask the chief from the old man's nation of people to say a few words in recognition of what I truly believed in as this is what the old man truly believed in as well. Do this as I am raised," Tree pleaded.

"More importantly," Tree added, "You must guide our modern- day cowboys and Indians into a mutual understanding of interest and friendship. Between themselves and the land they both share to walk on together. You can do this, Georgy, just as the old man taught you how to treat people."

Georgy agreed to both requests. Then he granted Tree to his heaven. Away from the boundaries made from broken trust. Eagle watched in despair as Georgy, in an effort to bid a final farewell, took a last look at what was left of the smouldering hole in the branch. A sudden shiver ran through his entire body.

Suddenly, the sky exploded with thunder again and the rain eventually snuffed out the fire that had so badly singed Tree. It couldn't have come at a better time as Georgy would have perished in the flames, too.

"I realize the wisdom behind the voice from within this tree. I also know that there is no fate but what we create ourselves. I will only say that I will try, Eagle, to do my part in looking after our world the best way that I know how."

"You must convince many that this is the moment for change, before the Spirits get angry again."

For the next few weeks, Georgy stayed pretty close to home reliving the events from the fire on the mountain, while trying to come up with a workable solution as to how he should go about undertaking such a task.

STOP THE CLEAR CUTTING

Seventeen

A Season of Change

Georgy knew it could take years before people would begin to listen. He also knew he had to do whatever he could to stop any further destruction. Before he knew it though, summer had come to an end and it was time to hit the school books again.

So back to university he went. Georgy formed an ecological support group and spoke at town hall meetings, telling of the hazy air above them and of the acid rains that were dropping all around them.

Georgy eventually challenged the government to stop clear-cutting the forests. He told of contaminated water surrounding their region due to industrial waste and of the fish that were no longer edible as a result of it.

Things seemed to be moving slowly just as Georgy expected they would. He knew Will would tell him to keep on trying, so that's just what he did.

Georgy graduated from university a few years later. He had finally become a Licenced Conservation Officer. Staying within the government enabled Georgy to convince them to clean and restore the neglected mountain parks and trails nearby.

Georgy closely monitored campfire usage in campgrounds. Through tiring convincing, government agencies like Lands & Forests all began to jump into action.

A Native Heritage Support Group was started, utilizing the wisdom of the Indigenous people from town and nearby reserves, to construct a heritage resource centre that would also include a museum.

People were hired to restock fish levels in nearby lakes and to tree plant neglected bare spots along the neighbouring mountainsides. Then they tackled the older buildings in town, fixing up and painting them in an effort to clean up the entire area that they lived in. People took interest in the new changes and the word quickly spread to many towns and cities across the province. Others followed Georgy's ideas and before long the general feeling between all people involved was of great self-awareness and proud accomplishment.

Before long word had spread to other cities Canada-wide. Nationally, government subsidized programs were implemented for farmers to start new crops, while locally, new water and sewage treatment programs were introduced to the townspeople and business owners. Industrial plants were made to use clean burning incinerators, as well as to have their own waste treatment programs upgraded. Public burning, garbage disposal and water usage were cut back in an effort to conserve wherever possible.

In no time, these programs were being implemented everywhere in the country. Georgy was called upon in other towns to speak about the progress that had been made. In every case his message was the same. Georgy plan had been both thoughtful and deliberate. The land began to start taking shape through this planned awareness. Georgy said that it boiled down to needing the efforts of many to begin to work together in order to produce positive results.

PART III
Creating the Totem

Eighteen
Back Home

Georgy kept in touch with Eagle whenever he was back home. He had a mirror he would use to reflect the sun up to where Eagle was. This would signal Eagle that Georgy wanted to talk to him. Georgy kept moving the mirror around until he noticed the big bird circling high above. In a few minutes Eagle would be by his side.

"Welcome home, Georgy. You have been a busy man lately," Eagle said.

"Good to see you, Eagle. Busy, yes, but there's more to do still," Georgy replied.

"Georgy, it is not the same without Tree anymore. The only company I have is that silly Raven. He had the gall to try to build a next in Tree's branches now that Tree can't yell at him."

"So, what did you do, Eagle?" "I yelled at him and told him to find another location, that there was only room for one nest, and that this one was mine." "It's time to pay attention to Tree.

This is why I've called you. I wanted you to know what I'm planning to do," Georgy said.

"I can't wait to hear, Georgy."

"I've asked the Chief of the local Band if he would consider meeting with me to discuss a proposal. He said he would, so I'm seeing him this afternoon. If all goes well, we'll have a plan in effect by the end of the day."

"Georgy, I am confident that all will go well. You are asking the right person. I am sure that with what your intentions are, he would only be too happy to be a part of it."

"My plans for the totem are a little out of the ordinary, but nevertheless meaningful."

"Would you care to fill me in, Georgy?" Eagle asked.

"Not until after the chief and I have met," Georgy replied. "Just in case he doesn't approve. I wouldn't want to get your hopes up too soon."

"I understand, Georgy. Good luck today. Please keep me informed."

"I'll signal you right after the meeting," Georgy said. "It's time for me to get going now, Eagle. We'll talk later."

Eagle took off toward the mountain. Georgy watched and thought of how happy Eagle would be when he would learn of his plans for the totem.

Soon it was time to meet with the chief. Georgy jumped in his truck and drove to the nearby

Reserve. There he found Chief finishing up a meeting with the Elders of the Band Council.

When the Chief noticed Georgy he beckoned him to come in.

"Hello Georgy Walker. Welcome," Chief said.

"Good afternoon, Chief," replied Georgy. I'm glad you could see me today."

"I understand you have a request to present to me."

"Yes, Chief. My proposal is simple. I propose we construct a totem pole out of the tree on the edge of the ledge up on the top of that mountain there. I am led to believe that is on the border of Crown and Reserve land."

"This totem, what is the reason behind you wanting one? What shall it commemorate?" asked Chief.

"Your Fathers and their Fathers before them would go to the ledge, to tell stories and wait for the Spirit Gods to appear. It is the very tree out on that same ledge, the one with the hole through its branch, that was the favourite of the old man and the site that he spoke so highly of when he was alive."

"Georgy Walker, why do you feel you should undertake such a task?"

"I was very fond of that tree. Tree, Eagle and I spent many days together up on that ledge. I learned more from Tree than I could ever tell you."

"How do you think you can achieve this task, Mr. Walker?"

"I come to you for your help, hoping that you would carve the totem using the five symbols that were critical in the planning of the work that was done in aid of our planet Earth."

"Do you have a design in mind, or a sketch?"

"Yes," replied Georgy. "This is not traditional but it could mark the start of a new era in our lives."

Georgy showed the chief the drawing he had made. The chief studied it, asking what each symbol represented.

"It is my plan to have the trunk of the tree as a base, a War Chief next, then an inquisitive, young boy climbing towards the top where a magnificent eagle stands guard over all things below it. And finally, on the top, a perfect circle hole which would represent a window in the world that when looked through would show off Mother Earth's beauty."

"These other symbols, Mr. Walker, who might they represent?"

"The trunk is the tree's own. The Warlord Chief is the old man from the reserve, the young boy is me and the eagle is the friend that still lives in the tree on the ledge. These symbols would represent the few good people that truly cared enough to want to change the world to make it a better place to live in. It would also be a reminder to all that saw it to stop and think about what it represents."

The chief discussed the plans with the Elders in their native tongue for a few minutes, then looked back at Georgy. "You want us to carve such a totem?" asked the chief.

"Yes. I respect your people. The old man was very dear to me. I had the utmost respect for him. After all, it was his request to have our people respect each other, and to do a complete turnaround in terms of treating our earth the way we always should have been. was he who was most like a father to me, and I feel this is the least I can do in his honour."

"This will be a very unique looking totem, Georgy Walker. The old man was my father. He said many good things about you. He would have been proud to see what a difference you have made here so far. I would be happy to carve your totem. We have decided to let it stand on the mountain ledge. I will go to the tree tomorrow and we can discuss how best to begin."

Georgy was elated and shocked to hear the Chief was Will's son.

"Thank you, Chief, and thank you, Elders," Georgy said. "I will keep in touch with you over the next few days." Georgy shook the Chief's hand and left to tell Eagle the news.

Georgy summoned Eagle as soon as he got home. Eagle again noticed the reflection from the mirror and flew down to Georgy right away.

"How was your meeting, Georgy?" Eagle asked.

"It's a go, Eagle. The chief has agreed to fall and carve the totem. He appreciated my reasons for using the symbols I've chosen. I basically told them that the special design would represent the similarity in friendship we shared personally between us and that it would stand for the ongoing hope we have in upholding the beauty of our world we share together."

"Tree would have wanted me to do this, and I'm sure Will would have appreciated my reasoning. After all, he was a good teacher."

"So, what happens next, Georgy?"

The Chief will go look at Tree tomorrow and then fall him. They will begin right away.

It will take about two months to complete. This will give me time to make arrangements for the day when the totem is raised."

"Georgy," Eagle began. "I know you must have wondered many times why it was you who was chosen to carry on with this work. Once, when you were a small boy you acted very mischievous. You decided to play with matches." "One day you started a fire in the woods behind Will's cabin. If it had not been for Will that day, the forest would surely have gone up in smoke. You acted just like Raven. Tree was aware of this, and so were the Spirits when they set fire to the mountain, killing Tree."

"I guess they wanted you to feel how they did when a single tree gets cut down or burned.

But now, through your hard work, you have shown everyone how you have turned a sorry situation into one with positive, new beginnings. You have made up for your carelessness as a child. Tree knew all along that you would follow through with making a big difference here.”

“Well, it doesn’t stop here, Eagle. There’s a lot more to be done. I’d better get going on this. I’ll stay in touch. You’ll see the chief up there tomorrow.”

Georgy watched as Eagle headed for home. In the next few days that followed, Georgy and Chief agreed on a design. Then it was time to fall Tree. They decided to start the following morning. The next day Georgy made his way up to the site. He watched as the men worked at chopping the tree down. Not long after, it came crashing down, coming to rest just a few feet from where he had stood.

The carvers immediately began cutting the branches and skinning the bark from the tree. The other men began to make a covered area from planks and plastic that they had hauled up the mountain over the past few days.

Word of this event soon spread throughout the valley. People from town came to watch the carvers begin their work. The chief began by covering the totem front with paper and sketching an outline drawing over the areas that they would carve.

Georgy was amazed at how much time and effort went into the carving of the pole. It was exciting to watch the carvers start their work, and to watch as Tree slowly began the transformation into a totem.

Chief took time out to talk to Georgy about possible arrangements that would have to be made in preparation for the totem pole raising.

“We will provide a ceremony around this event,” Chief said. “We can discuss the details later, but there will be a feast and dancing.”

“My idea,” Georgy said, “is to promote awareness to as many people as possible through the raising of this pole. I intend on inviting the radio and newspaper people to help spread the word.”

“How can my people be of assistance, Georgy?” Chief asked.

“Your expertise and supplying the right amount of people will be most important. I’m going to need horses to transport people up and down the trail, and men to lead them. We’ll need water

and hay. We’ll need some tarps and a large tent. I’ll look after getting some tables up here for the food and I’ll rent a portable outhouse for our guests.”

“Okay Georgy,” Chief said. “I’ll make the necessary arrangements when we’re closer to being finished.” “I think that will be just great, Chief. Thanks for the offer. Yes, we’ll definitely need to coordinate this closer to the time. Will the totem be protected up here as it is being worked on?" "I have arranged for some of my people to take turns staying here until it is completed," the chief assured Georgy. "We are building a better work shed for more protection as well."

"I'm happy with where we're at, Chief. Things are beginning to take shape. What kind of time are we looking at to finish the totem?" Georgy asked.

"I'd say a couple of months, Georgy. I want to pay close attention to the detailing before we begin painting." "I can see it now, Chief. I've envisioned it standing there since Tree died." "The time will quickly pass, Georgy. I had better get back to the pole now and give somebody else a rest."

"Thanks, Chief, for all that you're doing." "It is my pleasure, Georgy. See you later," Chief said.

Over the next few weeks, Georgy focused on the radio and newspaper groups, telling the story of this challenge to the local community and other towns and cities to clean up the land. Georgy's work had already impacted council members all over the place. The newspaper and radio interviews helped spread awareness, keeping everyone informed of his progress.

It got to the point where everyone was anxious to meet Georgy and couldn't wait to see this totem pole that he was having constructed. He was by far the most popular Conservation Officer around. People came from all over to listen to him talk about his accomplishments, above and beyond his job. He was certainly becoming admired and highly respected for the work he was doing.

The weeks seemed to fly by. Georgy kept in touch with Chief to ensure things were still running smoothly. One morning Chief asked Georgy to meet him in town.

"Hello, Chief," Georgy said as he arrived at their meeting place.

"Good morning, Georgy Walker," Chief replied.

"How are things going up on the mountain?"

"We are right on time. Actually, the carving is complete. I think you will be happy with the work that's been done."

"It's been six weeks since I've been up there," Georgy said.

"A lot has changed in six weeks," Chief said. "We begin painting today. I would like to show you what I think for the pole colours."

"I can't wait to see it, Chief," Georgy said excitedly. "How about we meet at about noon?"

Georgy suggested. "That is fine by me, Georgy," Chief answered.

"Good, then we'll see you up the mountain later," Georgy said as he turned and headed for home.

Georgy couldn't stop thinking about what he thought the totem would look like. Already he imagined how awesome it would look, towering over the valley below. When he finally arrived home he beckoned to Eagle.

As usual, a few minutes later Eagle flew down and landed beside Georgy.

"What would I ever do if the sun weren't shining and I had to get hold of you? There'd be no reflection for you to notice," Georgy said.

"I will have you know, Georgy, that I can see whether you are wearing boots or shoes from my perch up there. I credit myself with having a good pair of eyes," Eagle bragged.

"Good. Next time I'll just wave my arms around and you'll know to come, right?"

"Sure. Try it next time. Don't worry, I'll see you," Eagle said. So, what's up, Georgy?"

"I met with Chief just now. He told me the totem has been fully carved. He wants me to meet him up there at noon to look at it. Then they want to begin painting. I'm so excited, Eagle. It's been a long time coming."

"Great news, Georgy. So am I finally going to be able to get a look at it now?" asked Eagle.

"I think it's time. I need for you to share in the excitement, too. After all, you're a big part of it, Eagle."

"Am I a symbol on the totem, Georgy?"

"Yes you are, my friend," Georgy answered.

Eagle was silent.

"What's wrong?" Georgy asked.

"I'm honoured that you would include me as one of your symbols, although I do not feel that I symbolize anything much, Georgy. Does this mean that you will tell me what else will be on the pole?"

"How about joining us up on the mountain at noon so you can see for yourself?"

"I would like that, Georgy. It has been hard to imagine what has been carved when I only get glimpses through the plastic."

"I think you'll agree that Tree would be happy when you see the work the carvers have done, Eagle."

"I truly miss Tree," Eagle said sadly.

"So do I, my friend. I'm sure we're doing the right thing. This is in his honour, too, you know."

"Thanks Georgy," Eagle said. "I will watch for you at the top. Make sure Chief and the other carvers expect me so I do not get yelled at or something."

"Don't worry, Eagle. They all know who you are. They've been anticipating your arrival for some time now."

"You don't say," Eagle said. "If I had known that I would have perched on their covered area and watched them work. I think that for now I will just wait for you and Chief to get there. See you soon, Georgy."

"Okay, Eagle. We won't be long."

Eagle took off. Georgy went inside to rest before setting foot up the mountain. He knew that in another week the totem would be completely finished. Now they could finally begin the ceremony planning around the totem pole raising.

Just before noon Georgy set out for the mountain top. By the time he reached the top, Chief was already there, awaiting his arrival. Just then, Eagle flew in and landed beside Georgy.

"You finally show yourself, Eagle," Chief said.

"It's my fault you didn't meet earlier," Georgy said. "I was keeping the carving a secret in hopes of surprising him at the last minute."

"Well, it is an honour to finally meet you," Chief said.

"I did not want to get in your way," Eagle said.

"Actually, you would have made for some good company up here. You are an important person in what we are doing, you know."

"So I hear," answered Eagle. "I am anxious to see what you have done."

"So am I," Georgy added.

"Well, step this way," Chief said. "We were waiting for you to get here."

Eagle and Georgy followed Chief over to the covered area where the totem sat. When they walked through the door, Eagle hopped up onto Georgy's shoulder. Georgy was elated. The carving was perfect. The symbols were almost lifelike.

"Tremendous job," Georgy said to Chief.

"What do you think, Eagle?" Chief asked.

"This is absolutely amazing. I had no idea that this was what you had in mind when you first talked of a totem pole, Georgy."

"This is exactly what I'd wanted, Eagle. The symbols represent the main characters involved in making a difference around here," Georgy said. "Shall we discuss painting them now, Chief?"

"Sure," Chief replied.

Together they talked. Eagle stared in admiration of the work they'd done in carving the totem. After discussing the colours to be used, Georgy and the chief went over the last minute preparations for the ceremony.

"My people want to supply the food for the feast," Chief said. "They are excited and proud of what has happened around here lately. Everyone wants to help. The drums will soon echo in the valley, Georgy. My people will begin building the scaffolding tomorrow."

"Okay, Chief. I'd like to watch them, to be a part of the preparation. We'll see you tomorrow. Thanks again for all that you're doing."

"It is my pleasure, Georgy. Go rest up. You will need a good night's sleep if you are going to learn to build a scaffold strong enough for a totem raising."

"Okay, Chief, I'll take your word for it."

"See you tomorrow, Eagle," Chief said.

"I am looking forward to it. I am impressed with what I see. I can see the delight in Georgy's eyes, too."

"Let's meet at ten tomorrow morning, okay Eagle?"

"Sounds good. "I will see you then. Bye for now, Georgy."

The three friends quickly parted company. The following day Georgy again hiked up the mountain. By the time he reached the top he was surprised to find that the tribesmen had already assembled two tri-pod stands made from poles they had carted up the mountainside. Bound securely together with strong ropes, these would act as the scaffold stands. A crossbar would be placed over the top, between the two stands, enabling the men to throw ropes over to begin hoisting the pole up.

"Sorry I'm late," Georgy said to Eagle perched over by the men. "You're right on time. These men started work hours ago."

Just then Chief came out of the covered area. "The day is half over, Georgy," Chief kidded. "You should know that from your fishing days.

 "Looks like they've got a good jump on the day," Georgy replied.

"There's still a lot to be done," Chief said. "My men will use a series of levers and pulleys on multiple riggings before raising the pole. For now, Georgy, you might help by digging the deep pit that the totem will be set into. One of the men will show you where to start. After that, large rocks will have to be packed into the base to protect the pole from being uprooted by the strong winds and to allow for drainage so the pole won't rot. Smaller rocks and dirt will have to be thrown on top afterwards to fill up the hole. You might as well get started, Georgy. You will be busy today. We had all of the rocks dragged up by the horses."

Georgy did whatever he could, trying not to get in the way. By late afternoon the pit was done and the men had finished building the necessary riggings. Heavy ropes would have to be brought up as well, but all in all it looked as though they would be right on time for the weekend ceremony.

Georgy decided to pop in on Chief and the others working on the totem. "Hello men," Georgy said upon entering the covered area.

"Hi Georgy," Chief said. "Have you had enough for one day?"

"It's fascinating watching these men work. I'm amazed at the heart and spirit they possess while working." "It is an honour to be part of the traditions of old. They are happy, Georgy. They eagerly await the pole raising. They know that soon they will take part in the ceremony."

Georgy decided he would stay away from the mountain. For the next few days he wanted to reflect on his fond memories of Tree and to relate what this whole project meant. He too, waited with eager anticipation at seeing the totem completed but wanted to be surprised at the final outcome of the experience.

The morning before the ceremony, Georgy tried to summon Eagle but he never showed up. A little worried, Georgy set foot up the mountain to look for Eagle. He had also wanted to meet with Chief to make sure they were ready for the next day.

When he got to the top he found everything in place just as Chief had promised and to his surprise there was Eagle, sitting beside Chief, just outside the covered area.

"Hello my friend," Chief said. "We have been expecting you."

"I hadn't wanted to bother you, Georgy," Eagle said. "I knew you had a lot on your mind."

"I got a little worried when you didn't answer my call," Georgy said. "I thought your eyesight was getting the best of you," he kidded.

"I was merely keeping both eyes on the developments around here," Eagle said.

"Are you ready for tomorrow?" Chief asked.

"I am ready and excited. How about you. Chief?"

"My people have everything prepared. Would you like to see the totem?"

"No, Chief. I'd like to wait until tomorrow."

Chief nodded, "We will meet in the morning to await the arrival of our guests."

"I'll phone around to make sure everyone's ready, rain or shine," Georgy said. "I can't believe it's finally time."

"Believe it, Georgy. We can't wait to erect this totem. Your dream is our dream. It means a lot to us. Go rest up, Georgy. We will meet tomorrow."

"Did you remember the horses and water, Chief?"

"All taken care of, Georgy. Everything is going as planned."

"Looks like it's finally going to happen," Georgy said to Eagle.

"Wait until you see the totem, Georgy, it is beautiful."

"I can hardly wait," Georgy replied. "So, Eagle, how about meeting me in the morning? I'll rehearse the speech I'll give tomorrow. You can tell me what you think."

"Sure," Eagle said. Let me know when you are leaving. I will watch for your signal."

"Okay," Georgy agreed. "Now I'd better get busy. I still have to finish the speech. I'll see you in the morning. Everything is going to work out just fine. It will be a great day tomorrow."

"Goodbye, Georgy," Eagle said, as he flew up to the mountainside.

Georgy made his calls to the media. Everyone was coming. He then sat down to finish his speech. A lot went through his mind. He was happy with his accomplishments so far and knew that in time everyone would benefit from the hard work that had been done by all.

The next day saw Georgy up early and whistling to himself. At breakfast he went over last

minute details in his mind, and then headed out the door to signal Eagle.

In a matter of minutes Eagle arrived. "Good morning, Georgy,"

"Good morning to you, Eagle," Georgy replied. "What a beautiful day. What's it like on the mountain?

"The horses are feeding at the bottom of the path. It's a buzzing atmosphere up there. Wait till you see for yourself. Everything is ready. So, where is your speech?" Eagle asked.

"It's right here," Georgy said, patting his shirt pocket. "I've decided it would be best to let you wait to hear it. I hope you don't mind Eagle."

"No I don't mind Georgy. I trust your judgement." Eagle said.

As they began their hike to the top, Georgy reminisced about the days when the three of them used to talk together up on the ledge.

"It is really not that long ago since Tree left us, Georgy."

"Today he will live again, this time forever," Georgy said.

Halfway up the mountain Eagle noticed that Raven was watching them. "There have been a lot of people up here lately," Raven complained. "I liked it better when there was nobody around. It is all because of you, Georgy Walker."

"No, it's because this town needed a gentle nudge to open their eyes to a more appreciative way of living," Georgy challenged. "I'd venture to say that even you Raven, will benefit from the change that is happening. Just wait and see."

Georgy and Eagle continued on their way. When they got there they noticed a big fire pit burning in the middle of the clearing. People were busy cooking and setting up for the feast.

Georgy commented on the huge rigging set up. Ropes and levers were in place, ready to be put to the test. Large rocks lay to one side, ready to be thrown around the base of the totem.

Just then the chief emerged from within the covered area. "Good morning, you two."

"Hi Chief," Georgy said cheerfully.

"It looks like we are ready for our guests. We are all set to go, Georgy. I have wrapped the front of the totem so you can have an unveiling. That will keep everyone in suspense and

will help protect the totem from getting scratched from the ropes when hoisting."

"What's left to do, Chief?" Georgy asked.

"Absolutely nothing, Georgy. Just relax and greet your guests when they arrive. My men will take their places when it is time."

Admire the totem,
but always remember
this tree's sacrifice
Stay inspired...
dare to dream

Nineteen
A New Era Totem

To Georgy's surprise people began arriving almost immediately. Little by little the clearing began to fill up with town folk, invited media and members of Chief's band. They were all here to watch the ceremony.

Soon the time was upon them. As the crowd mingled about, Georgy gave Chief the wave that they should get things underway. Chief responded with a nod. Eagle flew up to the roof of the covered area to watch, as Georgy called out to get everyone's attention.

Georgy welcomed everyone to the ledge. He introduced himself and then, as originally promised to Tree, turned the dedication over to Chief to say a few words on Tree's behalf.

Chief spoke, "Today we take part in a new beginning brought about by the efforts of one

individual who has prioritised caring for our town and surrounding area, making it a better place to live. His influence was that of a single tree on this ledge, who spoke out to this man"

"It took desire, courage and focus for this man to climb up this very steep hill, never once thinking to quit his struggle as he pressed onwards, seemingly un-phased by the obstacles that lay in his path. When he finally reached the top he learned to become a listener. He found from this tree the sense there would be in prioritizing a plan for our future co-existence. This man is with us today. It gives me great pleasure in recognizing you, Mr. Georgy Walker. The crowd clapped as Georgy thanked Chief for his kind words.

Georgy spoke, "Today we bless a new era totem. I do this with great honour. This totem will stand for all people to recognize the symbolic significance it holds for us in three very important ways. The first is for the First Nations Elders. Through their wisdom and courage may they forever continue to uphold their traditions of old. Secondly, for the friendship we proudly share between us and thirdly, for all the gifts Mother Nature lends to us daily. May we never abuse the privilege of borrowing from her beautiful abundance ever again."

Georgy turned and hugged Chief. As the crowd clapped, Chief motioned for his men to begin moving the totem. The door to the covered area opened. About thirty of Chief's men slowly began making their way out, carrying the totem. When they reached the rigging, they gently set it down onto a large log just ahead of the open pit hole, in position to slip the heavy ropes around it. Others sprang into action. Two sets of long ropes were thrown over top of the scaffold crossbar and were placed around the upper part of the pole, to keep it from swaying left or right. There were at least a dozen people at each of the rope ends.

A skid plank was set inside the pit to assist the pole in sliding in easier. Chief took his position beside the pole to direct the pole raising. When he gave the word, the men pulled on the ropes. As the pole began to lift up, other people took position manning a log crutch they had made for the pole to rest on in between the stages of raising.

Inch by inch it was skidded into the pit. Chief played a very important role by directing everyone cautiously as they worked.

It was a slow process but you couldn't afford a single mistake. Georgy was elated to be witnessing such a sight. To think that a tradition as old as this was still being used today, gave Georgy a sense of how proud the people raising the pole must be feeling at this very moment.

Excitement filled the air as the burlap covered pole drew nearer to being up-righted. The dream that someday the pole would be erected was finally a reality.

The height of the totem was twenty feet. It was just perfect size. When the pole reached its upright position, everybody clapped and cheered. Men began packing the large rocks into the base as the others kept tension on the ropes to keep the pole stabilized. Earth was then thrown over top of the rocks, filling up the rest of the hole.

When the men were done, Georgy hushed the buzzing crowd. When all eyes were upon him, Georgy went over to the pole and pulled on the rope that held the wrap around the totem. As the burlap fell to the ground a feeling of elation filled Georgy's heart. Chief looked over at Georgy and smiled, acknowledging his happiness.

It was certainly different from any other totem he had ever seen, but then it was supposed to be.

Respect was definitely the focus of this whole experience, but Tree and Will were the ones who Georgy thought of at this very moment. Now they could rest.

A tear rolled down Georgy's check for Tree would have been proud to see what he'd been transformed into. After a few moments Georgy collected himself and continued on with the dedication.

He began by thanking Chief and the carvers for their beautiful craftsmanship displayed on the totem and for the countless hours of hard work the people donated to the cause, for without them, there would be no celebration at all.

Georgy ended by thanking everybody for attending. "I assure you," Georgy added, "you have all helped make this a memorable moment in my life. Now I believe it's time for all to partake in a celebration so please stay and have some fun."

The scene suddenly came alive with drumming as reporters scurried about taking pictures. Chief and the other carvers began dancing around the pole, their tools still strapped around their waists, while the women tended to the open pit fire where the venison for the feast had been cooking.

Eagle flew down to Georgy. "Was it like you thought it would be, Georgy?"

"Oh yes, Eagle. It is so beautiful and so colourful. I can't wait to get close enough to feel it."

The crowd mingled around the totem. Chief came over to talk to Georgy.

"I'm glad I waited until the totem was erected to see it in its entirety. I'm both surprised and truly thankful for what you did for me, Chief."

"It was my pleasure, Georgy. You did say, we have all come a long way together."

"I have some gifts for you and the people who worked so hard on this project," Georgy said. "I've arranged for some engraved medallions and monetary gifts to be given out before the feast starts. This is a very proud day for me. I'm so delighted that my dream could be included in so many other people's lives."

"You have left a good impression on all who attended. It will soon spread to everyone, thanks to the newspaper," Chief said.

"It is time to start the feast, Georgy," Chief said as he hurried off toward the covered area.

Georgy walked up to the totem and scrutinized the symbols on the front. It truly was a work of art.

Almost immediately, people came together to begin eating. The drumming got more intense. Chief's people began to dance and chant. It was a spectacle to see. Now Georgy and Eagle were content just watching. The food was plentiful and the people were certainly being entertained, but as the hours flew by, late afternoon grew quickly upon them and Georgy thought he should start to head for home.

Everyone had been fed and a good time was had by all. Chief's people began to clean up. Georgy called for Eagle to join him over at the pole. Eagle landed on the top of the totem.

"You look good up there, Eagle," Georgy complimented.

"I thanked Chief for that earlier," Eagle replied. "This pole will make for some great company up here, Georgy. It is as though Tree is alive and with us again."

"He is," Georgy confided in Eagle. "He'll be with us forever now, my friend."

After the ceremony was over and most of the people had gone, Georgy and Eagle stood staring in admiration of the totem. A few minutes later, Georgy noticed Chief sitting quietly by himself over to one side of the ledge. He too, had been watching the totem.

"Thank you, Chief. You really said it all with your speech. You know it is you that is teaching these people. You've touched the hearts of everyone who came here today. It's a noble thing wanting to lead these people the way that you do."

"My father was a proud man. He chose to live alone for reasons of peace. He too kept busy teaching and did so right up until the day that he died. You were his most important student."

"So, is the reason you stare at the totem, because you see your father in it?" Georgy asked.

"Your new era totem is quite interesting," Chief said. "The objects you chose to use are in fact symbols of a very important family. Our family. Yes, I knew who the chief symbol was meant to represent and I want to thank you again, my friend. I respect your friendship. My people will look after everything. They will use the horses to carry the heavy things down tomorrow. So, keep in touch. We will see you again soon, Georgy."

Chief gave Georgy a hug then left to make his way home.

"Georgy, you look as though you have something to say," Eagle said.

"Tonight, I will sit back and reflect on the steps we took that got us here. One dream I had as a child was to climb this mountain. Another was to become part of looking after it. I've completed both of these childhood dreams by living them out from the start. If I could have one more dream come true, Eagle, could you guess what it would be?"

"To build me a nest inside the hole at the top of the totem?" Eagle asked.

"No, old friend. You may nest with me up in the barn if you'd like. Besides I still enjoy your company."

"What would you wish for Georgy?"

"I'd wish for people everywhere to go after their dreams, no matter how large or small, and to never give up hope that someday they might, through some kind of encouragement, become inspired and begin to live with a more positive attitude, leaving discouragement behind."

"I'd hope they could learn of my dream and experience my encounters, to learn what a difference one man, a tree and one mountain made, not just to my life, but indirectly to everyone who was here today," Georgy concluded.

Georgy looked up at the totem. "What a difference you've made in my life," Georgy exclaimed. He turned to Eagle, "It's time for us to go home, my friend." "You made a lot of people believers today, Georgy, and I sense that this is only the beginning."

"It took some convincing, but I think I've finally become a believer in myself," Georgy stated.

Twenty
Mayor for a Time

About twenty years passed since Georgy first climbed the mountain. During that twenty years he travelled the country as a Federal Conservation Officer consulting in setting up programs, policies and procedures where needed and overseeing them until they were completed.

The years seemed to fly by and soon enough Georgy's time with the government was up. He retired from his job and began wondering about what he should do for the next few years. He heard the Mayor's position was up for election and that the current Mayor would not be running again. Lots of people told Georgy he should run, so he did and won.

For the most part people respected Georgy. The town had long since grown to be a city that had honoured him with a plaque around the time the totem was erected, as a thank you for all his hard work he had done. Georgy gave the mountain path a name, "Wildheart Trail", a name Will had given to him as a younger boy.

Well, so much for the fun stuff. Being Mayor didn't turn out to be as easy going as he thought it would be. One of the first things that was expected of Georgy to do was to solve all the problems of the area in and around the city.

"Mayor Walker," said one of the Aldermen. "One of the reasons you are in the position you are, being Mayor of our fine city, is because of your skill at being able to work out difficult situations pertaining to city and rural affairs, keeping within the allotted budgets. Now I see we have other situations arising which, if not stopped, could be out of control in no time flat. I don't think that trying to solve these problems is going to be easy on you."

"If you're referring to the clear cutting around the valley, there's not a lot I can do about it. We are dependent upon the logging industry. It employs about one half of the working people in almost every town in this province, not to mention the export trade business we do. It's too important to our economy." "Before running for Mayor, you were highly respected as a man of integrity, with solid morals and a keen understanding of all issues around you. You resolved the issues keeping fair play in the forefront at all time. Now the public cries out for the trees in the forest. To cut them down will only lead to the destruction of the natural watershed our valley boasts of having, not to mention the animals who will suffer. Just for the money, Mayor Walker?" the Alderman asked. "Suddenly I'm seeing conflicting principles."

This caused Georgy to sit and stare into the wall ahead of him.

"So, what is right, Mr. Alderman?" Georgy asked. "I don't like it any more than the next person, but we've got to do what we have to do, don't we?"

"I'm just trying to remind you of the man that fought so hard to right the wrongs done by so many before him."

It was at that moment Georgy Walker decided he could no longer be in the Mayor's position any longer.

"You're right, Alderman. I'm as guilty as all of the rest who get caught up with the money wars that seem to forever dominate our lives. It's so easy to forget about what really matters the most. We're dependent upon our Mother Earth, yet we keep abusing her at every chance we have to make a dollar, so that we can continue to exist on her soil, under our terms. Thanks for holding me accountable to what I truly believe in," Georgy said sincerely. "Besides, with the cutbacks in budget trimming, I was sure to have to look at canceling some of the projects I'd created. I'm obviously fooling myself by being in this position."

"What would you do with yourself?" the Alderman asked.

"I think I should lay low for a while. Besides, I could use a rest. Maybe I'll write a book. I could always start a recycling program or something. It might save some of the trees out there. I know just the spot on a certain mountain where I could write without distraction. Besides, I want to stay on the good side of the Spirit Gods. You don't want to mess with them."

(Back at home with grown up son, Taylor)

"So, you see, Son," Georgy said, "there were many concerns that even I couldn't fix to make everyone happy. You know, sometimes I think back to what I'd seen through the hole in the branch so many years ago. How about I take you so you can see for yourself?" Georgy asked

Admire the totem,
but always remember
this tree's sacrifice.
Stay inspired...
dare to dream

Twenty-One
Grand Finale

Georgy and Taylor set out for the mountain. He needed to see how the totem was holding up anyway. The Parks Branch had really done the mountain justice. They had the road paved, complete with a parking lot near the top. They had even created a lovely pathway that wound its way to the ledge, with a sign that was labeled 'Wildheart Trail'.

Georgy decided that he and his son would walk the trail. As the pair approached the ledge, an all too familiar voice rang through Georgy's mind. The fenced look-out had a sign that read: 'Use caution! Stay away from the ledge!' And there stood Totem, proud as could be. Together they stood, just as before, only this time, Tree did not speak, but then he didn't have to.

"Taylor," Georgy said, "If we don't start looking after the Earth little by little, it will be taken away from us. Tree was taken but not before he passed along some concerns he had about saving the world for our fellow mankind."

Georgy had a ladder mounted to the back of the totem so that everyone could climb up to look through the hole at the top. "Go ahead, Son," Georgy coaxed. "Climb up and have a look at what the Eagle guards every day."

"Hey Dad, there's a plaque mounted here at the top. It's to you. It's a lifetime achievement award. It says, 'You had it in your heart, you kept an open mind. You spoke in sound advice, you cared to help mankind. From the citizens of Lake Cowichan. That's awesome, Dad!" exclaimed Taylor.

Georgy felt proud to have been able to give Tree something back in return for his teaching. But it took everyone to be a listener. Now it would be up to everybody to do the best they could, every day onward.

"Let's say goodbye to our friends on the totem, Son," Georgy said. "I'm sure that in time you'll get to know them a lot better."

Georgy smiled as he put his arm around Taylor's shoulders. As they walked away, Georgy turned to once again notice how truly awesome the totem looked against the beautiful, landscaped scenery of the valley below.

"It's really awe-inspiring up here, Dad," Taylor said. "Let's stand by the fence and look down into the valley.

"Taylor, when I stand up here, the memories I have of Will are so vivid, at times I think I can hear him calling out to me. He will always remain a big part of my conscience. Look, there's my house, Son."

"We're as high as the clouds up here," Taylor shouted.

Georgy stood for a few moments and thought of how interesting it must have been for a tree to be able to watch over a small boy from such a distance, especially when that same small boy lay daydreaming of a time when he could be a part of being up there with the clouds.

Georgy looked across the valley to the mountains facing him when he suddenly became aware that there was a face-like image, resembling that of Will, etched into the rock face of the mountain side facing him.

"It took a while, Taylor, but now I know what Will meant when he said 'you won't easily forget about me, Georgy'".

Taylor looked up at him and said, "Dad, in a way you've grown up to be like Tree, Eagle and Will. You knew them really well."

Georgy smiled and said, "It took the characteristics of all of them to mold myself into the person I've become today. Good or bad, what matters the most is the inspiration they gave to me, and the change they've helped make in my life. I feel that I have been blessed."

At that moment tears welled up in Georgy's eyes. They slowly began to trickle down his cheeks. They were not tears of sadness, but tears of joy.

Georgy nudged Taylor and said, "Let's make our way back, Son." A gentle rain began to fall but that was okay because rain kept the surrounding area fresh and clean and that was a good thing.

Twenty-Two
Lessons of Inspiration

(Georgy in a field napping with his dog)

Georgy, still asleep, dreamed that a light drizzle was falling down around him. Tiny drops rolled down his face. As he wiped the rain from his eyes, a familiar bark awakened him.

Georgy sat up and rubbed his eyes. At that point he realized he had been vividly dreaming, and it wasn't raining either. He'd been lying on his back in the field as Ben eagerly licked his cheeks and eyes in an effort to get his attention.

"Ben, how long have we been sleeping?" Georgy asked. "We'd better go home before we get into trouble. We've been gone for hours."

Georgy yawned and stretched. He looked up and saw the Eagle circling high around the clouds over the mountain top. He wanted now, more than ever, to get to the top of that mountain.

Georgy was glad to see that nothing had changed. He was still ten years old and had his whole life in front of him.

"Nothing's going to stop me now, Boy. Let's go see if Dad will take us up there for a hike this weekend."

Desire had already filled Georgy's heart as they scampered off across the field. Only time would tell whether or not Georgy would be influenced by the dream he had in the clover field that day. Would it affect his life? For now, he was inspired enough to at least want to start living out one dream. To climb up to the top of that mountain and touch the clouds, just like Will had.

- END -